H

so he could w

the bottle on

noticing she was wearing a pair of pointy high heels. Damn. She looked good in anything she wore. He couldn't help think she looked great in everything that was underneath too.

In an effort to get his mind off her curvaceous figure and avoid the embarrassment of being caught staring, he said, "So where did you learn to cook?"

Rebecca opened the broiler and turned the pork chops. "Television." She placed the fork on the spoon rest and covered the cooked carrots with foil. "What's so funny?"

His laugh was husky and low. "That's where I learned. I'm surprised Liz hasn't bragged about my culinary skills by now."

Rebecca smiled. "She has mentioned you make one mean marinara sauce."

He shook his head. "Leave it to a kid to only remember spaghetti sauce."

She held out a wooden spoon filled with salad greens she had just tossed for him to taste.

When Travis' tongue flicked over his lips, her knees went a little weak.

"What is this dressing? It's delicious." He took the spoon from her hand and ate the remainder.

When he licked his fingers, she groaned inwardly.

"Homemade vinaigrette," she answered weakly.

Travis handed her the wooden spoon and the tips of their fingers touched. Hers tingled. Now more than ever, she knew whatever barrier she had thought she put between them no longer existed. God help her.

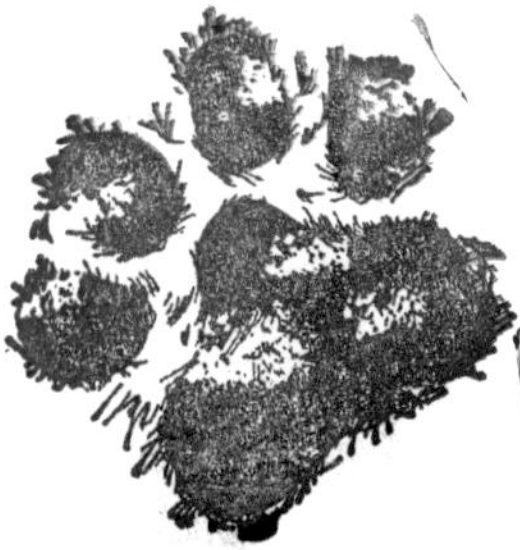

Self defense classes

All my best!
Cathleen Kelly

Training Travis

by

Cathleen Tully

Training Travis

Contact Information: info@thewildrosepress.com

Cover Art by *Tina Lynn Stout*

The Wild Rose Press, Inc.
PO Box 708
Adams Basin, NY 14410-0708
Visit us at www.thewildrosepress.com

Publishing History
First *Last Rose of Summer* Edition, 2013
Print ISBN 978-1-62830-166-3
Digital ISBN 978-1-62830-167-0

Published in the United States of America

Dedication

To my biggest supporters,
my husband Joe and my daughters,
whom without I would truly be lost.
Thanks for pitching in when I'm on deadline and
helping make my dream as a published author possible.
Love you all always and forever!

Chapter One

Rebecca Evans kicked the driver's side tire on her white commercial van, which currently looked like an overcooked pancake—the tire not the van. Most days, if she had her way, she rode her bike. It was healthier and definitely safer.

She hated cars—and only drove when necessary in order to transport fabrics, wall coverings or other samples to and from client appointments for her interior design business. Or, like this morning, when she wanted to return the truck to its parking spot right outside Designs of Distinction. It had poured yesterday afternoon, and finding herself minus an umbrella, she'd driven the van home, then returned this morning—only to discover the pancake of the century.

She gave the cell phone an impatient tap of her index finger while Walter Grimms, the local mechanic, chuckled at her predicament. "How many flats does this make, Becc? Three in six weeks? You should have bought that new set of tires when I told you to." He laughed. "Stay put. I'll be right there."

"Thanks." Rebecca disconnected the call. Oh, he was a real comedian, all right. *You should have bought that new set of tires when I told you to.*

Easy for him to say. Walter's business had boomed after the expansion of his garage earlier this year. He had even hired more help.

Rebecca silently scolded herself. Jealousy got a person nowhere and she could learn a lesson or two from the older man. An honest man who never cheated anyone, if the mechanic said she needed new tires, she needed new tires. Too bad her bank account wasn't bigger. Yes, she had enough money to buy the tires—but there would be little left afterward. For things like rent, food, utilities.

She gazed up at the beautiful skyline of the Poconos, a mecca for tourists dead center of the great state of Pennsylvania, that surrounded her hometown of Golden. The sun shone brightly on this crisp December day and a cold breeze blew her shoulder-length hair into her eyes. In an habitual gesture, Rebecca pushed it behind one ear.

She inhaled and let the fresh air fill her lungs to the point where they almost burned from the extremely cold air. God, she loved this town. She'd never felt so close to nature as when she was here in Golden with its multitude of many-colored trees and mountain bike trails. In the spring and summer she was an avid hiker. During the winter months, she was an avid skier.

As she tossed her phone into her purse, a gray SUV pulled to the curb behind her van. A man jumped out and after slamming the door shut, swaggered down the sidewalk in her direction. Something about him seemed familiar. She squinted to gain a better view. When he drew nearer, recognition pulsed at a mind blowing pace.

Travis McGill.

Years ago, when she'd have sworn they would be together forever, when she believed in love everlasting, when she'd memorized every detail about his appearance. Looking at him now, she couldn't believe how much he had *not* changed.

His six foot three inch frame still looked lean and though she wasn't close enough for an up close and in person testimony, likely just as hard as it had been as a teenager. With deep brown hair, short and combed straight back and eyes that same chocolate syrup brown, at eighteen, he'd been the most handsome boy at Golden High. His All-American good looks, combined with little-boy cuteness, had most of the girls doing cartwheels—though their fawning and flirting earned them no success.

Back then Travis had eyes only for Rebecca.

And she'd returned that adoration ten-fold, envisioning their future together—complete with children in a cozy little home, living happily ever after.

Until he crushed her dreams and broke her heart.

Today he wore black: cowboy boots, snug denim jeans that stretched in all the right places—and cupped in the righter ones, a slate blue cashmere sweater, and a gray down vest. While she checked him out he shoved his hands into his pockets and studied her.

Feeling slightly lightheaded, she took a step back and leaned against her van, blaming the sudden feeling of lightheadedness on lack of protein and caffeine. There had been no time for breakfast this morning—not even a cup of coffee. Still, all the protein and caffeine in the world couldn't have prepared her for this moment.

Fifteen years ago he left for college at Rutgers University. With both sets of parents constantly telling them they were too young to become serious, she and Travis agreed to see other people while they were apart.

After all, school was four hours away and the

chances of seeing each other more than once a month were slim. So, he left Golden and Rebecca stayed. By the time Thanksgiving arrived, Rebecca knew trying to live without him wouldn't work. While he was home for the holidays, they ran into each other at the local post office and their gazes locked. She'd melted into his arms like the last piece in a jigsaw puzzle and from that day, they were inseparable.

The day Travis left to return to school, they said goodbye, promising each other they'd call frequently and not let so much time pass before they saw each other again.

But when Rebecca didn't hear from him, she called him at his dorm. He was in college, after all, class work and tests must have had him bogged down. Or so she thought.

Travis' roommate answered the phone and told her Travis had left school abruptly. The first thing Rebecca did was check with his mother who claimed not to know anything about her son leaving school. Rebecca left his house feeling terrible that she'd alarmed his mother but, honestly, she hadn't known what else to do. Two weeks later she learned Travis' mother had also left town.

A few months later Golden's rumor mill cranked up to announce he moved to Chicago and his mother had followed. Rebecca never really knew the person who circulated the information and never bothered to find out.

Instead of pining, she'd picked herself up and concentrated on getting on with her life. After four years at Philadelphia's School of Art and Design, she graduated with a certificate in Interior Design.

Her vow to rid Travis McGill from her mind had worked.

Until now.

****

"Becca?"

At the sound of the pet name he called her years ago she found her heart beating unusually fast. She couldn't speak; all she was able to manage felt like a simpering, weak-kneed nod.

Travis removed his sunglasses and smiled.

Those brown eyes sparkled as he slowly took her in—one inch at a time. A tingle spread throughout her body. His gaze managed to melt her like an ice cream cone on a hot summer day. "How have you been?"

She pulled her coat closed tightly around her torso and refastened the sash. *Until now, fine, thanks.*

Travis leaned in and kissed her on the cheek.

Her body tensed. Her mouth dried. She closed her eyes in an effort to regain control. When she inhaled, her heart fluttered inside her chest, his musky aftershave reminded her of the times she had worked so hard to forget.

Over the years she pushed all thoughts of Travis McGill from her psyche. She even convinced herself the adolescent obsession with him was over. She went on with her life and met Mike. They dated, married and started something of their own.

Now, seeing Travis in the flesh, feeling his lips on her cheek and smelling his special cologne had doubt bolting through her at lightning speed and her legs wobbling like strands of soggy spaghetti.

Travis gestured at the flat tire on her van. "Need a hand?"

Fifteen years too late, buddy.

She cleared her throat. "No." Holding her hand above her eyes she squinted when she looked up at him. "My mechanic is on his way. He'll be here any minute." *I hope.* "What I need is a cup of coffee."

Nauseated by the sugary way her voice squeaked, the last thing she'd wanted was to sound like a lovestruck teenager, but God help her, she felt seventeen all over again.

Travis' laugh came all the way from his size twelve boots. "Some things never change. You still a java-holic?"

The fact that he hadn't blocked all memory of her likes and dislikes didn't impress her one bit. Millions of people drank coffee. Big deal.

He gazed down the road and pointed. "I think your mechanic's here."

Good. In a very few minutes, she could leave and they would say goodbye.

Walter Grimm's parked his flatbed in front of Rebecca's van.

Travis went back to nibbling on the frame of his sunglasses and for a moment memories flooded her mind like an avalanche. Holding hands by Morgan's Lake, making out at Peter's Peak. Her eyes fell to Travis' lips. One thing she would never forget about this man; he had been a fabulous kisser.

She blamed the chill that ran through her on the weather. A blast of December air caused a bunch of dry leaves to circle around their feet.

Walter's voice snapped her from her daze. "Want me to change the flat here or bring it back to the station?"

When Travis grinned at her she felt her cheeks flush with heat. *Great. He had caught her staring at his lips. Suave, Rebecca, very suave.*

She turned to face Walter. “No. Please bring it back to the station. And I’ll take those new tires we spoke about last week.”

“Okay.” The older man smiled and rubbed his chin. Then he turned to hook her truck up to his flatbed.

“I’d be happy to give you a lift,” Travis offered.

“No thanks. I can walk.” *Oh, yes, a walk was just what she needed to stay focused.*

“It’s no problem. I have time.”

“I only work a few blocks from here.” Rebecca craned her head and looked around. “And it’s a beautiful day. Besides, I like to walk.”

She pulled her cashmere scarf tighter around her neck and shoved her gloved hands into her coat pockets. Right now, she wished more than ever she’d taken her bike to work this morning. But business was business and advertising cost a lot of money. Driving around town in the van with Designs of Distinction plastered over the side garnered more business than any newspaper ad would. Plus, if she had ridden her bike instead of driving, this entire incident with Travis would have been avoided. Six of one, half a dozen of another, she told herself. What’s done is done.

“I’ll walk with you.”

She wanted to ask him why he was being a persistent pain in the butt, but didn’t have time for trivial conversation—with Travis McGill or anyone else. She had more important than wasting time talking to someone who was unimportant to her.

The steady stream of clientele brought in small

jobs that turned around quickly and the profit not always as large as she would have liked. She needed to build a nest egg for when business became slow—for times like this when unexpected car repairs became necessary.

And she'd promised herself that over the coming year she'd increase her clientele by at least twenty-five percent. Budgeting and allotting money for advertising were priorities she needed to address before this year was over.

During the last few years in business, she had put some money aside but certainly not as much as she should have. If she obtained a few larger design jobs with the profit margin earning more than just window treatments, her emergency account would grow faster.

What she could really use was a commercial job. Better yet—a large renovation that would take months to complete. Oh yes, those kinds of jobs would help keep her bank account healthy and her books in the black.

Rebecca started across the street. When she reached the sidewalk she turned. "Travis, I really have a long list of chores which need my attention today."

He didn't answer. Instead he nibbled on his sunglasses again.

Hadn't he learned how to do anything else in fifteen years?

He shot her one of those amazing smiles and for a moment she almost forgot where she was headed. A horn blared shaking her from the daydream. She almost sprinted across the street when the light changed. Maybe if she walked faster he would take the hint. But no matter how fast she walked Travis didn't seem to break a sweat. Four of her steps equaled one of his. She was the only one perspiring from her power walk.

At the next traffic light they waited for the green signal. A school bus packed with teenagers on its way to Golden High School drove by. Laughter and loud voices filled the uncomfortable void. Travis touched her elbow in an effort to guide her safely across the street; she pulled out of his hold.

She blamed the shiver on the temperature dropping drastically since she'd left her condo for work this morning. A large snowstorm had been forecasted for the coming week. Living in the mountains had its pros and cons. She should have worn her heavier coat but after oversleeping, she'd hastily grabbed this one in an effort to get the day started. She wouldn't make that mistake again. No one knew better than her what a bear Pennsylvania winters could be. The last thing she needed was to catch cold, or worse, the flu.

And let's not forget coffee. Rushing to be on time was useless if she skipped coffee. A good cup of coffee would really hit the spot about now. It would also snap her out of this daze she seemed to have fallen into. A brisk winter wind smacked her in the face. She flipped up the collar of her coat and buried her hands back into her pockets.

At the next corner she made another attempt at getting rid of her elusive shadow. "We should say goodbye here. Although it was nice seeing you again, I have a busy day ahead." She offered her hand to Travis in a businesslike fashion, but he ignored her.

"I'd like to spend some time with you, Becca. I thought perhaps we could talk."

Spending time with Travis was the last thing she

wanted. Coffee was the only thing she needed or wanted right now, and Travis McGill could walk to the ends of the earth, barefoot or hog-tied, for all she cared.

They walked past *Kate's Café*, a small coffee shop frequented by locals. The front door swung open, wafting the aroma of freshly brewed coffee and hot muffins right out of the oven under Rebecca's nose. Her stomach growled. She turned away from the wonderful fragrance and willed herself not to stop.

Although Kate's coffee was known for its rich flavorful body, just what she needed to sharpen her senses this morning, she had coffee at the shop and could brew a pot when she got there. She also had low fat blueberry muffins she'd purchased a few days ago in the small refrigerator in the shop's tiny kitchen.

Her mind buzzed with a list of things she had to get done today. Custom shipments that arrived yesterday needed inspection before they could be installed. There was a ton of merchandise that had to be priced, shelved and stocked, and numerous phone calls to be returned.

In an effort to stress the urgency, she quickened her pace. "I really must get to the shop."

Travis followed. "Okay, we'll talk there."

"Aren't we talking now?"

Rebecca tried hard to make her voice sound light and airy even though her stomach had balled into a knot. *What had he expected from her? A warm, loving greeting? Jeez. Men could be so dense.*

She came to an abrupt stop in front of the shop and fished in her oversized purse for her keys.

Travis glanced in the window. "You work here?"

Nodding toward the entrance, she located the key in the bottom of her purse. "I *own* here."

When he still showed no signs of budging, she pushed the door open with one hip. The door was ancient and the damn thing always stuck. She made a mental note to hit it with some DW40. The bell above the shop entrance rang as they walked inside.

Travis followed her in and closed the door behind him. When Rebecca turned to face him, her mind went blank.

Great.

Travis looked around. "Nice place."

"Thanks."

He stood there like a statue with his hands in his pockets. Rebecca sighed. Fine if he didn't intend on leaving, she'd just go about her business. Sooner or later he'd take the hint.

She walked to the rear of the shop and draped her coat across the back of her cushioned desk chair, then turned her attention to the coffee station. Travis fidgeted with his car keys and she found the jingling sound unnerving.

"What brings you to town?"

Get him in. Get him out. Pronto.

Rebecca turned and Travis' hand was on her upper arm. She blew out a deep breath and looked him right in the eyes, removed his hand from her shoulder and let it fall. "What is it about the whole personal space issue that you don't understand?"

He didn't reply, just smiled at her.

Those eyes again.

For a moment they melted all rational thought from her mind. Damn, but she had forgotten how mesmerizing they could be. It irked her that his mere proximity could still rattle her.

"What do you want, Travis?"

This man managed to awaken all her senses and tick her off at the same time. She swore if he touched her again, she might just kick him.

Hard.

Travis stood so close she could feel the warmth of his breath on her face. She inhaled deeply in an attempt to clear her head. It didn't help. What had he done this morning? Bathed in aftershave?

She took two steps back and felt the coffee station counter right behind her. A few seconds later the aroma of brewing cinnamon hazelnut coffee beans filled the air and Rebecca instantly relaxed. She turned to watch drops of legal stimulant drip into the glass carafe, mouth salivating at the thought of her first sip.

Okay, so she was a java-holic. Dealing with Travis now, she'd probably exceed her usual three cups and finish the rest of the pot all by herself. Damn, he irritated her so much she might even eat two of the three muffins in the fridge.

"I'm moving back to Golden."

Her mouth dried.

Moving?

Back?

Here?

Who the hell did he think he was to show up out of nowhere and upset everything? She'd worked hard to make a life for herself—a life that did not include Travis McGill. His announcement deflated every ounce of energy from her body. She leaned back into the cushioned chair. How she wished she had powers that could transform her out of her shop and back to her warm, sheltered bed.

Briefly, she thought about asking him why he had decided to return to Golden after all this time, but quickly changed her mind. She no longer cared. Travis' reasons were his own. And they didn't concern her.

So she turned her interests back to the coffee station relieved to see it was done brewing and the carafe was full. She breathed in the lovely aroma of cinnamon and hazelnuts emanating from the machine and filled a generous mug to the brim.

When she turned to face him the smirk that had been on his face a moment ago quickly faded. Rebecca gripped the steaming mug so tightly she thought it might break. And he was standing much too close again. Irritation roiled deep in her stomach; she gently pushed past him.

She detested surprises—especially early in the morning. However, she knew no matter when Travis had given her this news, it would not be the right time. She would never have welcomed his return to town.

Travis glanced at her mug of coffee.

The butterflies in her stomach turned to vicious bees on a mission to escape. Staring at the mug filled with coffee, she contemplated running an IV directly into her arm, but since she took her coffee with cream and sweetener that wouldn't work.

She added cream and sugar and retreated to her thickly cushioned desk chair awaiting any further bombs Travis felt the need to drop on her this morning. With coffee in hand, she could handle anything.

She hoped.

He pulled up a chair and sat opposite her.

Would he never leave?

Travis rolled his wrist and checked his watch. He

wore something sleek and expensive. He must do pretty well in whatever field he's in.

"I should get to the airport. Let's have dinner later this week."

She swore his eyes pleaded. Didn't he just say he was moving back to Golden? If that were true, why was he headed for the airport?

Rebecca took a sip of coffee then shook her head. "Can't."

"Any day. You pick."

"I'm busy."

"All week?"

She nodded and sipped again from her cup of sanity. Truth be told, she'd rather shove splinters under all ten fingernails than share a meal with this man.

"What about this weekend?"

"My calendar is full on Saturday, and Sunday is *my* day." She had no time to play nicey-nice with Travis McGill and wasn't about to give up a Sunday for him—or anyone.

"Golden is a small town. People are bound to talk." He kept his voice low and played with the car keys he had extracted from his pocket, jingling them to an intolerable level.

So that's what this was all about? This urgent need to talk had nothing to do with her. It was all to avoid gossip and the possible effects it could have on his future business here in Golden. He was merely playing damage control. She closed her eyes and blew out a deep breath.

He had to be the greediest man she had ever known. Instead of answering, she stood and started toward the door. Gripping the handle tightly she swung the door open wide for him. "Didn't you say you had to get to the airport?" The look Travis shot her advised he didn't believe one word she'd said. "Do you ever get tired of life revolving around you?"

He shook his head. "It's not about me, Becca. It's never been about me. It's about—"

She put her hand up and stopped him mid-sentence. "I don't care. We're adults. I'm sure we can manage to live in the same town. I know I can."

Rebecca checked the clock on the wall above the antique cherry armoire, grateful for the passing of time. "Don't you have a plane to catch?"

Travis blew out a deep sigh and walked over to where she stood. "Please, have dinner with me when I return?"

Perhaps if they'd parted differently so many years ago she might have consented to meet with him.

Perhaps if he'd manned up and been honest—even given her the benefit of a flipping phone call...

Karma sure is a bitch.

Rebecca nodded toward the door. "I'm busy. Have a good trip."

"We will talk, Becca," he said and strode out the door.

****

With Travis on his way to the airport to do God knows what, Rebecca tried settling in for a full day of work. She slit open one of the waiting boxes with more vigor than was necessary and when blood dripped from her finger, she stuck her finger in her mouth and rummaged through her desk drawer for a bandage. Once secured, she returned to her task and pulled plastic-wrapped draperies from the cardboard box, then placed them on the antique Louis the Fourteenth chair she'd nabbed at a local flea market a few years ago.

What kind of person left everything and everyone he knew with no notice, then returned fifteen years later as though nothing had happened?

For the rest of the afternoon, she threw herself into the To-Do list on her desk. As far as Travis McGill was concerned, she'd shelve him and his reasons for returning to Golden in the alley behind the shop along with the rest of the trash.

Chapter Two

A little later that morning the bell above the shop door rang out and Leigh Evans swept into the shop as if she owned the place. “Hellooooo.”

“Mom.” Rebecca hugged her tight and inhaled the familiar scents of vanilla and jasmine, her mother’s signature scent, Captivate.

Leigh returned the hug with vigor. “Sweetheart, is something wrong?”

“Nice to see you too.” Damn. As it had been her entire life, maternal radar went to red alert at the worst possible times. “How was the cruise?”

Her mother slipped out of her knee-length cashmere coat, folded it in half, then in half again, and took great pains to lay it over the back of the nearest chair. Her medium brown hair sported red highlights and was cut short with bangs to frame a pair of big brown eyes.

“You know that’s not how I meant it, dear. You work much too hard. And as far as the cruise went, one week wasn’t enough.”

For today’s visit, her mother wore black straight leg slacks with a pale yellow angora sweater and a pair of black patent leather pumps with at least five-inch heels. Leigh never wore high heels.

Hmm. Here was something to consider. Her mother rarely made changes to her hair, claiming she wasn’t afraid to get old and liked the gray and white strands in her dark hair that almost looked like highlights.

"One week might not be enough, but you certainly seem rejuvenated. You look different, Mom. You're almost glowing. Does this new aura have anything to do with your dying your hair or buying those high heels?"

Glancing down at her shoes, Leigh turned an ankle in a model's coy pose. "Pretty, aren't they? I bought them while I was away. The pointy toe is in."

Rebecca's brow wrinkled. Why is she taking so long to tell me about the cruise she couldn't wait to go on? Rebecca's father had been afraid of large bodies of water, so her mother never raised the subject of a cruise while he was alive. Rebecca would have sworn when her mother returned she'd be a complete and utter chatterbox.

"Is there coffee?" Laughing loudly, Leigh walked over to the brew station. "What am I saying? My daughter the coffee addict always has a fresh pot."

Rebecca leaned against the antique cherry desk she'd treated herself to a few years ago, nodded and crossed her arms over her chest, waiting for a response.

Leigh blew on the hot coffee before sipping slowly. "Oh, this is good."

She then crossed the room to sink luxuriously onto a plush oversized chair, taking care not to crease her slacks. She glanced at the department store circular on the side table Rebecca had dog-eared. "Doing some shopping?"

Rebecca swayed from side-to-side. Was she intentionally avoiding looking at her? "I need a new suit and Rosenblatt's is having a huge sale."

Why isn't she telling me about the cruise she

waited over twenty years to take? The same cruise she'd lain awake the night before departure because she'd been too excited to sleep?

"I need to do a bit of shopping, too," Leigh said. "I could use new panties. Something with lots of lace."

Rebecca swallowed hard. Lace underwear? This from the woman who claimed the full-cut cotton style were the only ones she wore. "I was thinking of going tomorrow."

"Oh good." Her mother clapped her hands together like a kid in school. "We can have lunch, make an afternoon of it."

Rebecca smiled, studying Leigh closely. Leigh was the best person to shop with because she never lied about fit or color. *If she takes one more sip of that coffee without answering me, she is going to regret it.* "Okay. So are you going to fill me in or not?"

Leigh's eyes were big and wide. "Fill you in on what, sweetheart?"

"Your cruise?"

"Oh, yes the cruise. It was wonderful. Just what I needed to relax."

Rebecca bit the inside of her lip in frustration. She loved her mother more than anything, but she could be such a brat. Rebecca strode over to the coffee machine for a refill. The wonderful fragrance of the hazelnut cinnamon coffee wafted around her like a wonderful cocoon. She sampled the new brand that she'd bought on sale and found it not bad.

"The views were phenomenal," Leigh continued. "The food delicious and the sex mind-blowing."

Rebecca sputtered coffee all over herself and the brew station. She pulled a tissue from the box on the counter and blotted her chin and her sweater.

Leigh's laugh was low and lusty.

"Sex?" Rebecca lowered her voice and glanced around to make certain they were alone and no one had entered the shop without her noticing. *Great, Mom's having sex and wants to share.* She pulled at the collar of her turtleneck and checked the thermostat, which to her dismay, read seventy-two degrees.

"You know, sweetheart, you should go on one of those singles cruises. I hear they're packed with men eager to fulfill your every need. And you haven't had sex in how long?"

"That's none of your business." Rebecca's sex life, no matter how non-existent, was her business and only her business.

"It's just that you're always so tense. You could really use some."

"We were talking about you."

Leigh laughed naughtily. "Oh, yes...the sex!" Her eyes grew wide. Placing her hand on her cheek, she puckered her lips. "Woooow. That's probably why you think I'm glowing."

"Please tell me you used protection."

"Of course." Leigh placed her coffee mug on an end table. "I watch the news and am very much aware of all the STD's and other things one can pick up from casual sex."

"Don't roll your eyes at me," Rebecca snapped. "It is an important question."

"Of course it is, and I love you for caring about me. But we're not stupid."

Rebecca nodded. "Who is the *we* in that last statement?"

Inwardly, she cringed. The words had flown from her mouth before she could stop them. She was screwed. Once started on any subject even closely related to sex she droned on like a broken record.

Rebecca opened the brown paper bag neatly folded on the counter, sat on the chair nearest the coffee station, legs wide apart, her head bent and breathed into the bag.

In and out. In and out.

Leigh walked over and rubbed her back softly. "Honey, are you all right?"

"Sure, Mom." *Just dying a thousand deaths.*

"I see you're still having those panic attacks. Have you spoken to your doctor about medication? You're much too tense for someone so young."

Rebecca glanced up from the paper bag. "I haven't had a panic attack in over eight years, but thanks for reminding me."

She'd moved from panic attacks to stress-related episodes after she opened the business. Her doctor said they were normal. Rebecca was an anal retentive organizational mogul and she could expect palpitations and dizziness whenever she felt overwhelmed.

And right now, her mother certainly wasn't helping with this sexcapades information dump. More times than Rebecca could remember, she'd asked her to keep information like this to herself. Apparently she'd been talking to herself.

Leigh blew out a loud, deep breath. "If you say so, sweetheart. Perhaps you should eat more protein."

Rebecca leaned back into the chair, arms crossed. "I eat just fine, Mom."

"Then it has to be the lack of sex."

Rebecca groaned and pinched the bridge of her nose.

"Benjamin Higgins is the man who changed my life. Rebecca, the man's techniques are life-altering. What he does with his hands alone—well, let me tell you."

Oh God. She resumed the paper bag breathing technique. "Good for you, Mom. They say it's a great stress reliever."

"Oh, yes, oh, yes it is." Her mother's face flushed as she ran one finger over her bottom lip. But when she stroked her neck slowly, almost seductively, and released an appreciative sigh, as though she were reliving a very intimate moment, Rebecca thought she was watching a scene out of a movie.

Time to change the subject.

"It's okay, Mom. I don't need any details." She tossed the paper bag into the trashcan and walked over to the box she'd been inventorying when her mother arrived.

Leigh fanned herself with a design magazine from the end table in the designated visitor waiting area. "Are you sure? Because I haven't felt this fabulous in much too long."

Rebecca cleared her throat. "Yes. I'm sure."

"That's too bad, sweetheart, because women need to be educated. Have you visited that website I told you about, Tammy's Toys?"

"No." Rebecca rubbed at the throb beginning in her temples. *This just wouldn't end. Her mother had given her the name of the website after watching an episode of one of those damn afternoon television shows that educates women about everything from increasing orgasms to do it yourself decorating.*

"How else will we know what we like when a man asks?"

Rebecca glanced around the shop searching for a reason to escape this madness. The customer waiting area needed to be tidied, but there wasn't a soul in the entire store—beyond her sexually sated mother and herself. When the phone rang, she sprinted across the room to answer it and nearly tripped over the area rug on the way.

A few minutes later, still on the phone, Rebecca watched her mother slip into her coat, then grab her purse off the chair. "Shopping tomorrow?" she mouthed.

Relieved to be alone, Rebecca nodded. She was half her mother's age and the only man warming her bed these days was a ten-pound Scots terrier with an ice-cold nose.

Of course she was happy her mother had enjoyed herself on the cruise. Leigh Evans had just retired from almost forty years of teaching at Golden High School and deserved to enjoy life. Still, Rebecca couldn't help being envious that she'd returned so relaxed, de-stressed and full of energy.

Hell, if that's what sex did to you, order me up some!

Not one who practiced casual sex, she'd only dated two men since Mike's death eight years ago. Losing her husband and daughter in a car crash had more than devastated her. It had taken her quite a few years to get back out there and date again. And even when she did her heart hadn't been in it. She'd never find another man like Mike, and she didn't have the energy or will to try. The first didn't last more than two dates because after the guy actually asked how long they'd have to date before they slept together. She pulled a ten out of her wallet, dropped it on the bar and left.

The second, a seemingly nice guy named Jake, her friend Michelle had introduced her to, was more interested in skiing and beer pong. They'd only gone out half a dozen times.

Rebecca let out a theatrical groan and grabbed her hair in clumps before looking up toward the sky. "I need to get laid!"

****

Around noon, Michelle Haskell, Rebecca's best friend, hurried into the shop. Dressed in a down-filled, knee-length coat with hood, a scarf wrapped around her neck two or three times, suede boots with fluffy stuffing peeking out, thick wool mittens, the only part of Michelle's body that was visible was her nose—she looked like Nanook of the North. "Damn, it's cold out rhere."

Rebecca took the last bite of the salad she'd ordered earlier and closed the plastic container. She washed the forkful down with a sip of diet cola and nodded. "That's what we get for living in the mountains."

Michelle sat opposite Rebecca and unbuttoned her coat. A swishing sound filled the space.

"Take your comforter off, stay a while. There's a fresh pot of coffee. Want a cup?"

"Ha Ha! This coat is warm."

"It looks like you took the down comforter off your bed and wrapped yourself in it."

Michelle blew on her hands. "Your wit is extra

irritating this morning."

The only pediatrician in town, Michelle had a great bedside manner and all the parents in town trusted her. A person just couldn't dislike her honesty and warmth—both qualities emanated from her the instant she met someone. Not only was she the only pediatrician, but winter was in full swing and runny nosed children no doubt filled her waiting room.

Michelle rarely dropped by during the day so the reason must be serious. "To what do I owe this visit?"

"Honey, I have news and I wanted to be the first to tell you so you weren't taken by surprise."

With her back turned to her friend, Rebecca couldn't resist rolling her eyes. Michelle always took the part of the big sister, trying her best to protect Rebecca from anyone and anything that might hurt her.

Still, Rebecca never got upset with Michelle because her friend's good intentions warmed her. She tidied up the coffee table strewn with samples she'd been coordinating earlier for a client.

"Stop that for a minute," Michelle said. "I need to tell you something."

Rebecca slipped back into the chair opposite Michelle. "What's wrong with you? Are you sick?"

Horrible scenarios raced through Rebecca's mind. Michelle had lost her mother to cancer three years ago. *Oh, please don't be ill. I can't lose you, too.*

Michelle closed her eyes for a moment then opened them slowly. Rebecca's heart beat hard in anticipation.

"Okay. I'm just going to say it...Travis McGill is back in town."

Rebecca tossed her head back and released a loud sigh of relief. "Is that all?"

Michelle nodded.

"Thank God. I mean, I already know." She carried the fabric samples to her desk, anything to avoid her friend's judging gaze. Travis' return was unsettling enough; she didn't want Michelle worrying, too. With a growing pediatric practice and a happy marriage to enrich her life, she didn't need splinters like Travis McGill upsetting the balance she'd achieved in her life.

Michelle bolted from the chair and followed her. "What do you mean, you know?"

Rebecca stopped and turned. She had a feeling when Michelle heard Travis was back, her big-sister, I'm-going-to-protect-you side would surface. Rebecca looked her friend in the eyes and smiled. "I. Know."

"How? And why didn't you tell me?"

Rebecca stretched and rubbed her neck. "I didn't have time. Besides, it's not a big deal."

"I'm glad to hear you say that."

Rebecca filed random wall covering books back onto the shelves. "Yup. I met him on Main Street when I got a flat. I was waiting for Walter to come and tow the truck." She walked back to the table and pulled out a chair for Michelle. "Sit."

"Another flat tire?" Michelle shook her head and sat. "Please tell me you bought the tires Walter recommended three months ago."

"Yes, I bought the tires, okay?" Rebecca filled a mug with coffee and creamer then she pulled a muffin from the fridge. Placing it on a paper plate, she brought it over and placed it in front of Michelle, who would no doubt inhale it and then race back to her office. This muffin would be the only thing she ate until dinner.

"Good." Michelle wasted no time and broke the

muffin in two. “So, what did he say?” Then she popped a piece into her mouth.

“He said he’d tow the truck to his shop and replace all four tires.”

“Not Walter, you idiot! Travis.”

Rebecca shook out her hands. She’d rather not have this conversation right now.

Michelle exhaled loudly and popped another piece of muffin into her mouth.

Rebecca rubbed her hands down the legs of her dress slacks, then slipped into a vacant chair. “I don’t know why you’re acting as though this is a big deal.”

Michelle’s voice was low. “Because he hurt you, bad.” She shook her head, her eyes small slits. “No one hurts my girl and gets away with it.”

She sat there like a cause to be reckoned with and Rebecca’s heart softened. What would she do without her dear friend? Still, she could take care of herself. Rebecca bit her lip and placed her hand over her friend’s. “I love you for caring and worrying about me. But Travis’ relocation isn’t an issue for me. I’ve moved on, remember?”

Michelle nodded. “I needed to hear you say it, that’s all.” She sipped from the coffee mug. “I don’t want him hurting you again.”

“Never going to happen. You know why?”

“Why?” Michelle wiped her mouth with a paper napkin.

“No one gets a second chance to hurt me.” Rebecca smiled. *God that felt good to say. Too bad she didn’t believe one ounce of it.*

Thirteen years ago, her mother introduced Rebecca to Mike Roberts, CPA and owner of a small tax practice one town over from Golden. She'd gone on their first date dreading every minute of a date with someone her mom set her up with only to be pleasantly surprised by his sweet, honest nature.

Three months later, they were engaged; six months after that, they married. One year later, Rebecca gave birth to their beautiful daughter, Annie. She and Mike had the perfect life.

Michelle nodded. "Whenever you get that look on your face, it breaks my heart. I know you miss them, Beck, but you really should get back out there. You don't deserve to be alone."

Rebecca barely heard her. Eight years ago, on their way home from the movies, Mike and Annie were killed by a drunk driver. Rebecca's heartbeat seemed to slow, almost stop momentarily.

"Hey, are you okay?"

Rebecca's mouth opened, but no words came out. She forced a smile—a mechanism she'd become a pro at since losing the loves of her life. "I'm fine."

Truth was, she'd never be fine. She'd lost the two people that had given her life meaning. Unless someone experienced the same, they just couldn't understand the empty lost feelings she coped with day to day.

"Don't give me that." Michelle balled the paper napkin up and tossed it in the garbage can. "Great. Now, I've upset you."

Rebecca met Michelle's sympathetic gaze. "No, you haven't. I'm good. I promise. I may have lost two people I loved very much, but I keep busy and my business is doing very well. My life is good."

After months of attending a grief therapy group, she'd come to see her life still had meaning and thrown herself into her business, the only thing left that made her truly happy.

"Okay, I'll give you that much. Your business is doing well. But your personal life? Not so much."

"Hey, Sherlock and I are just fine. Thank you."

Michelle rolled her eyes. "A dog is not a substitute for a man, Beck." She dropped her voice and wiggled her eyebrows. "You need a man...you need..."

God. Another talk about sex. "Sherlock is a man."

"Do you hear yourself?"

"Unconditional love and adoration is important no matter who it comes from, you should remember that."

A smile crept onto Rebecca's lips the way it always did when she thought of the dog she'd come to own by accident. In the past, she'd walked Sherlock, a black Scots terrier for Mrs. Akers, an elderly neighbor, whenever she was away. He'd even spent the night at Rebecca's a few times and the two of them got along famously.

Six months ago, however, when Mrs. Akers doctors notified her family that she'd have to go into a nursing home, Rebecca offered to take Sherlock in to live with her. There had been no hesitation on her part and the relief on Mrs. Akers' son's face told her all she needed to know. It was a good deed that would go a long way. She and Sherlock would do just fine together, and Mrs. Akers could have peace of mind knowing he was with someone who would take the best care of him. Now, months later, Rebecca found it hard to remember what her life was like without the wonderful dog. Sherlock gave her a purpose and made sense of her crazy existence.

Michelle's eyes grew wide as she checked her

watch. "Shoot, I've got to bet back to the office. Let's have dinner later this week, okay?" She shoved her arms back into her coat and wrapped the long scarf around her neck.

"Sure, Thursday night?" Rebecca asked. "Lucky Leo's?"

"Okay." Michelle turned before opening the door to exit. "By the way, I saw your mom on my way over. She looks wonderful. What's her secret?"

"Apparently an abundance of sex."

Michelle stopped dead in her tracks. "What?"

Rebecca swished her hand in front of her face. "I'll fill you in at dinner."

"Okay...happy hour is always packed with single hunks."

Rebecca's brow wrinkled. "Hey, you're married."

Michelle's voice rose and she hollered, "Yes, I am, but you, my horny friend, aren't!"

Travis' strong arms and deep brown eyes flickered through her memory and her stomach began to flutter. Rebecca smirked. "Great."

Chapter Three

On Saturday, Travis climbed out of the black SUV he'd rented at Chicago's O'Hare Airport, glad to be able to stretch his legs. He'd been in a car, then a plane, then back in a car for five and a half hours. With no room to stretch, nowhere to walk, his body ached for a long hot shower.

Upon receiving the news of his ex-wife Bridgett's death, Cecile, her sister, who lived across town, immediately went to stay with their daughter Liz.

Travis had traveled to Chicago for the wake and funeral two weeks ago and had promised Liz she could stay on with Cecile and Rick until Christmas break. Hell, it was only two weeks, and her remaining here with her aunt and uncle gave him time to complete the mundane but necessary chores that came with relocating to Golden.

As Bridgett's twin, she and Cecile had been very close. Over the past few months, she and her husband, Rick, who had no children of their own, helped Bridgett with transporting Liz to and from high school tennis tournaments, and Liz had grown close to the pair.

On the ride from the airport to Bridgett's house, he stopped at a red light and rubbed his neck. He couldn't get over how only two short weeks ago he had been reading the morning paper over a hot cup of coffee when the call came that informed him his ex-wife had passed away in a car accident. The shock had been deep and strong. Travis hadn't been able to shake the sudden coldness that bit him to the core. If Bridgett's death affected him so strongly, he couldn't begin to imagine how long it would take his daughter to heal. His heart raced when he thought about what the teenager had lost.

Ever since that phone call, all he could think of was how his life and that of his teenage daughter would change forever. Unable to sleep or do anything to help him relax, he'd read every parenting book he could get his hands on. Still, he didn't feel confident about taking over as a full-time father. How many changes could one kid adapt to in such a short period of time without flipping out?

Hell, he wasn't worried about himself. He could acclimate. But his daughter had been and always would be a creature of habit. And because of that he worried how his plan to relocate both of them to Golden would affect her.

He'd grown up wrapped in its small town warmth, and he knew once she settled in, Liz would come to love it as much as he did. His daughter's face flashed before his eyes, bringing him back to the present and the reason he had come here. Pulling into Bridgett's driveway, the surging eagerness to pick up Liz and start their new life together came to a screeching halt.

Melancholy slapped him in the face as he gazed at the sprawling brick ranch he and Bridgett had shared for three years before they decided to divorce. Bought in a foreclosure, they got the old house for a steal using money inherited from her grandmother as a down payment. Sadly, in a few weeks, the modest house that oozed charm and personality would be sold and the money put away for Liz's future.

Travis loved living here and had painstakingly taken his time renovating it. Ripping up worn carpets to sand and stain the wood floors that hid underneath, repairing pocket doors so they slid smoothly, replacing windows, scraping and repainting shutters. He'd done it all with dedication and love. The older home had persevered through decades of Illinois winters, yet still managed to hold its grand stature. He let out a loud sigh.

They'd spent many good times together in this house after Liz's birth. But hell, even he knew all the good times in the world couldn't save a marriage that never should have occurred in the first place.

Travis strode toward the front door. He hadn't been the only one who had worked hard on this house. Bridgett had also put much of her heart and soul into the home. Looking at it now, he couldn't help but appreciate the many examples of her creativity.

A Christmas wreath with a huge red bow decorated the wooden front door reminiscent of the Frank Lloyd Wright period; a duplicate wreath hung from the black lamppost that shown brightly next to the garage. Small red and white lights twinkled on the porch; eight silk red poinsettia plants decorated the entrance steps.

Travis jammed his hands into his pockets and cursed under his breath. What the hell was the matter with him? No *real* man noticed red bows and twinkling lights. At least no real man he knew. He figured that's what he got for marrying a floral arranger all those years ago. He took the front steps two at a time. Apparently Bridgett's knowledge of design and color had rubbed off on him. Until now, he hadn't realized just how much.

He glanced at three black wooden rockers that dressed the porch. He and Liz had spent a lot of time rocking on those old chairs. She loved being outside; always had. Biking, skiing, tossing a Frisbee. God, he missed those years when she was little and life had been so much simpler.

Before his finger touched the bell, the front door opened wide. A burst of warm air from inside the old colonial teased him. The heat must be on high. No matter his many attempts at insulating the windows and doors, this house had always been drafty. Illinois winters were harsh and bitter. Snow seemed to always be mixed with rain, and the dampness chilled a person to the bone.

Cecile greeted him warmly, dressed in blue jeans and a sweatshirt, with her red hair pulled up into a bun. She'd never looked her age. Her smile wrapped around him like a warm blanket on a cold night—reminding him why she had always been his favorite of Bridgett's siblings. Down to earth and honest to the core, Cecile never put on airs. What you saw is what you got and he respected her for that.

"Travis, how nice to see you twice in one month." Her voice was tender and low. "I only wish the circumstances were different."

After he took her into his arms, they embraced for a long moment. Travis knew Cecile was no doubt wondering how she'd get through the weeks and years without her sister. Spending time together was a natural as breathing for both of them. His chest ached with sadness for her.

On the other hand, Travis wondered how he would

deal with the new role of full-time father, and whether he would live up to Bridgett's parenting standards. He couldn't help feel he owed her that much. Liz, too.

When he released Cecile her eyes were filled with tears. Losing her sister who was also her best friend had ripped her apart. He wished there was something he could do for her.

"Come in." She briskly rubbed her hands up and down her arms. "It certainly is damp out."

Quickly he stepped through the door into the large entrance foyer. Bridgett's decorating talent once again apparent. Pale yellow paint covered the top half of the foyer while bright white wainscot dressed the bottom.

How could someone so young and talented be taken away so quickly? Travis tamped down his anger. The last thing Cecile needed was his rendition of life and the unfair blow they had received with Bridgett's death.

She crossed her arms and held onto her shoulders. "Elizabeth will be down shortly."

"Thanks."

They walked into the living room and he sat in a yellow chenille oversized chair that had always been his favorite. Running his hand along the chair's worn arm, memories of little Liz dressed in footy pajamas cascaded through him. He had read his daughter dozens of bedtime stories from this very chair. He couldn't believe how fast time passed.

Cecile placed another log on the already roaring fire. Loud crackles and snaps from the dry wood filled the room. She sat opposite him on Bridgett's well-worn yellow and blue floral sofa twisting a tissue into knots.

"How is Liz doing?"

Cecile kept her voice low. “The same as two weeks ago. Bridgett’s death was deeply shocking.” She blew out an uneven sigh and her chest quivered.

Cecile’s attempt at strength touched him. She should be sainted. Bridgett’s death had shocked her, yet she put her needs aside in order to care for her niece until school ended for the holidays. He reached over to place one hand gently over hers, “I’m sorry. I didn’t mean that the way it came out.”

She smiled and gave his hand a squeeze. “I miss her so much.” She fingered her wedding band, turning it round and round.

“Of course you do.” He knew Cecile’s heart was breaking despite how strong she tried to be. To make matters worse, every time she looked in the mirror the loss of her sister would forever rush back—the vision of her identical twin a memory she could never escape. Bridgett and Cecile’s commonalities went far beyond hair color. They shared the same eyes, expressions, and mannerisms, things makeup and hair color could never disguise.

Cecile took a moment, stared down at her hands, gathered her thoughts then lifted her eyes to meet his. “Elizabeth hasn’t been herself since the funeral.”

Travis listened closely.

“Most nights she doesn’t sleep, she refuses to eat, and is beyond irritable.” Her tone flat and lifeless. “Her doctor came to see her, gave her a look over, and told us that her actions are all normal and her appetite should return soon. Still, I would watch her.” She blotted her nose with a ratty tissue.

Comprehension dawned. “I know all about her friend’s battle with anorexia last year. Bridgett filled me in a while ago."

Cecile nodded. "Good. Not that I think there's anything to worry about. Until this, that girl had a better appetite than most men I know." Her grin only lasted a moment.

Travis leaned back into the chair and crossed his legs. For a moment the only sounds in the room came from the crackling fire and the quiet tick tock of Bridgett's antique cuckoo clock that hung over the stone fireplace.

"Be patient with her, Travis. Children, like adults, deal with death in their own way, in their own time. Half of what she says makes no sense. And the other half is said without any thought whatsoever. Bear in mind not to take anything personally. Her words are full of hurt and confusion."

"I will."

She slumped back into the chair. "Honestly, I can't blame her for feeling angry, although I disagree with her feelings of guilt. So many emotions for a young girl to handle all at once." She stared ahead, her eyes distant.

"Guilt?" Travis leaned in toward her, his fingers threaded before him.

Cecile nodded. "Elizabeth confided in me a few nights ago about how she thinks her mother's death was all her fault. You see, Bridgett was on her way to Elizabeth's tennis match when the car accident occurred."

Travis pinched the bridge of his nose where a mean headache currently settled over his eyes. "I mean, I knew Bridgett was in a car accident but..." He shook his head. "Poor kid."

Cecile nodded. "I started to think about that night in more detail after Elizabeth went to bed. Sis had called me from the shop before she closed up that evening. What I think is even worse for the child is that she and her mother argued earlier that afternoon. After closing the shop, Bridgett headed in the direction of Elizabeth's tennis match." Cecile's voice cracked. "Well, you know the rest."

Unfortunately he did. An out-of-control truck slid in the snow and hit Bridgett's car head-on. She had died instantly.

"Shorthanded at the shop, Bridgett didn't think she'd be able to make it to Elizabeth's tennis match on time. Elizabeth accused her mother of being more dedicated to her business than to her. Their last conversation was an exchange of harsh words."

"She couldn't have been further from the truth about Bridgett's dedication to her," Travis said.

She picked up the framed photo from the coffee table of Liz and her mother. "We know that. No matter how old Elizabeth tries to act, keep in mind—" She wiped the glass off with her bulky sweatshirt.

"She's just fifteen," he finished.

Cecile smiled. "You got it."

Her words of reassurance didn't serve to boost Travis' confidence level. He couldn't kid anyone. There was still so much he didn't know about his daughter.

The kitchen phone rang and Cecile excused herself for a moment. Travis glanced at the coffee table splayed with Christmas ornaments Elizabeth had made from her pre-school days. He picked up a wooden ring stretched with a stamp done in red paint of Elizabeth's tiny hand and held it against his. She was so small then.

Elizabeth may be older and taller now, but she'd always be his baby. Leave it to Bridgett to save everything their daughter had made, which only reinforced the thoughtful, loving mother she'd been. He picked up another that had been hand sewn by Elizabeth. He closed his eyes and inhaled. Visions of Elizabeth racing down the front path, with Bridgett in tow, leaping into his arms rushed through his mind. She'd been so excited to show him her surprise. The slight smell of cinnamon still lingered after all these years.

Cecile's reentering the living room brought him back to the present. "I've told Elizabeth that some things happen in life we can't explain and will never understand." Cecile shook her head. "But honestly, Travis, try explaining to a fifteen-year-old that her mother's death was meant to be, that fate works in painful ways." She paused. "The child looked at me like I lost my mind."

For the first time since he'd arrived, he noticed her red eyes. Travis' felt like someone had cut a gaping hole right through the middle of his stomach. He didn't think he'd ever stop regretting not having lived within a closer proximity to Bridgett and Liz all these years. Maybe things would be different now. Maybe he and his daughter wouldn't have to relocate after all. Maybe she could have continued to live in the home he knew she loved so much if he'd never taken that job with Rob and moved away.

But he hadn't had a choice. Out of work for almost a year after he and Bridgett divorced, when a college friend, Rob McPherson, called Travis looking for a partner in his contracting business, Travis jumped at the opportunity. Being unemployed didn't bide well with him. He was a parent who needed to provide Bridgett with child support. Travis also wanted to start a college fund as soon as possible for Elizabeth. Now he and Rob had a booming business throughout the tri-state area. But at what price had he earned his success?

Living out-of-state while expanding and improving his company had been hard on him and his daughter's relationship. Over the past year, they hadn't seen each other as much as they once did and that just about killed him, because he had vowed long ago, to always keep their relationship a priority.

"Don't doubt your parenting skills, Travis. Elizabeth loves you very much."

It was as though she read his mind. He met her gaze.

"Right now, Elizabeth is too angry to listen to any explanations anyone may have about life, and quite frankly—" Cecile fiddled with the gold cross hanging from her neck. "I myself am having a hard time believing all that mumbo jumbo myself."

For a moment Travis just stared at her. Of all the people he knew who had strong religious beliefs, Cecile rated number one. Never had he thought the day would come when she would admit doubts about her faith. Although she never pushed her religious beliefs on others, he knew she had always been a deeply spiritual person. For her to question a faith she so firmly believed in, more than worried him. At least she still wore the gold crucifix that had always been part of her attire for years.

Concern creased his brow. Now, more than ever, he was thankful Cecile had her husband Rick to lean on for support. Even the strongest people needed someone in times like these.

"Yes." She nodded. "Even I have doubts. But then I have never lost anyone this close to me. Except my mother." Cecile shook her head sadly. "You know how ill she had been. Somehow, death can be accepted when a prolonged illness like Mom's caused her to suffer for so long."

Travis nodded. She was right. No one enjoyed seeing a loved one suffer. Cecile and Bridgett had lost their mother to cancer when Elizabeth was only two years old. Travis remembered tending to her so the two sisters could take care of their mother's business and close out her estate.

Cecile continued. "But Bridgett's death just seems so cruel, so unnecessary. My sister was a good person—caring, generous, young. I don't know if I will ever be able to accept her death or understand it."

Cecile straightened her back—the consummate strong one, holding it together for everyone else, without a thought to herself. Travis hoped she let go of her need to be so tough once he and Liz left and she had some much deserved time to herself.

He watched her pull a pillow into her arms and toy with the fringe. Helplessness swept through him. He hesitated about moving to the sofa and putting his arm around her. Cecile had never been the touchy feely type. A hello kiss or welcoming hug had been her limit. Bridgett had been the outwardly lovable one of the pair.

Cecile continued. "Elizabeth will return to her old self again. It will just take some time. Thank goodness children bounce back fast." She gazed into the fire. No longer toying with the fringe on the pillow, instead she squeezed the pillow tightly to her chest.

Travis prayed the same held true for Cecile. Right now she looked as though she would never return to normal. He ran his hand back and forth along the arm of the worn chair. His daughter's sweet voice echoed in his ears, "Read me another story, Daddy, please?"

A moment later he looked up in awe. His lovely, daughter entered the room. It had only been two weeks since he'd seen her, but Travis swore Liz changed. The baby girl he once held lovingly in his arms seemed to mature overnight. Standing before him was a young woman dealing with a very adult issue.

Death.

A young woman he now had sole custody of every day, twenty-four hours a day. And for the first time since contemplating this change, he realized his fear went deeper than a few layers of skin. His fear reached all the way to his soul.

At five feet three, Liz wore her auburn curls pulled up. Her complexion mirrored a china doll's, her eyes a vivid green. His breath caught in his throat. His daughter was the spitting image of her mother.

Liz stood tall and erect as if she were a statue. As if she had the weight of the world on her shoulders. But then, she did, didn't she? Skin-tight jeans, a pink turtleneck that barely covered her delicate belly button, Travis stifled a groan. He couldn't remember if she had always dressed this way or whether he had just never noticed. He told himself, it didn't matter. Now was not the time to discuss wardrobe choices. Now was the time to be there for her and just love her.

He had more important issues to deal with such as the role he was expected to play and how he would handle this full-time father gig after only being a dad that saw his daughter two weeks a year and on weekends. He rubbed his sweaty palms on his jeans.

Liz stood with her hands in her back pockets—jaw jutted forward, her stare defiant and strong, a real cause to be reckoned with.

"Hello, Liz."

When he reached out to hug her, she folded her arms and walked stiffly past him to look out the picture window that displayed a playground of fresh snow that had fallen last night. Travis shoved his hands into his pants pockets. *Okay, remember what Cecile said, she doesn't know what she's doing or saying.* She does not hate you, his internal voice screamed.

Outside, neighborhood children made snowmen, slid down the steep hill on sleds and giggled, enjoying their snowball fights. Laughter permeated the glass pane. Clearly those children were having the time of their lives. If circumstances had been different, Liz would have been right out there in the middle of them. The most popular baby sitter on the block, she never hesitated to partake in snowball fights of any kind with the neighborhood kids.

But today wasn't any other day. Today was a day Liz would remember for a long time. Leaving the home she had grown up in and relocating to a town she'd never been to was clearly hurting her. No. Nothing about the past two weeks had been normal. And right now, Liz didn't even seem to notice the children playing happily outside. Her face had a far away look.

"Travis."

He bit his lip. Had he heard her right? Did she just call him by his first name? He shook his head to clear it. Okay, this was new. He conceded there would probably be many new issues he would have to deal with over the next few months, all of which would be foreign to him.

He folded his arms across his chest and took a few steps toward her. Travis wanted nothing more than to pull Liz into his arms and tell her everything would be okay. But every instinct he had, like the hairs on the back of his neck standing up in warning, told him to back off. He listened.

Liz turned to face him. Her icy glare could have frozen an entire swimming pool. "That is your name, isn't it?"

He forced a smile. "What happened to good old Dad?"

Travis hoped his light tone would help ease her out of what he could tell was one hell of a nasty funk. He had seen her in a mood remotely like this once before and didn't relish dealing with it again.

Last year when they had gone to upstate New York to ski she'd shared a similar mood with him. It had been very unpleasant to say the least. Not until he took her home the first evening from a day on the slopes had it been revealed that she had missed the freshman ball that Friday night. Bridgett hadn't liked the boy who asked Liz so she had concocted some lame story about how she had promised Travis that Liz would spend the weekend with him.

After he found out the truth, including why his daughter had been so unhappy all day, he made Bridgett promise to never again use him as a pawn in any negotiations with their daughter.

Liz turned her back on him. "You haven't been a

real father since you left Mom and me when I was three years old."

Ouch. Definite hit below the belt, as well as untrue.

"How can you say that? We see each other every weekend."

Liz stared down at her empty hands. "Not lately."

"Your tennis schedule has kept us apart." He pulled at the collar of his turtleneck, mainly to give himself breathing room. "I thought you wanted me to accept that, and we'd see each other when you were free."

What was with her? She was fully aware that after he and Bridgett divorced they had put Elizabeth's needs above all others. They had maintained a friendly relationship that allowed Liz the freedom to avoid parental arguments or disagreements over topics related to her. Come to think of it, he and Bridgett had never argued after their split. And on rare occasion, if they did, they made sure it was never in front of their daughter.

Liz blew out a deep breath and wrapped her arms around her torso.

Damn it. He hated taking the blame for being an absent parent. He wasn't the one who asked for the divorce. But now wasn't the time to discuss Liz's misinformation. In the weeks ahead he would have to learn to ignore many more comments like this. After all, she wasn't thinking clearly.

Truth was, he had been hurt when Bridgett requested the breakup. He had pushed his own wants aside, married Bridgett, and fathered their child. Determined to make their relationship work, he had thought they were making a real go of it until one afternoon, out of the blue, when Bridgett announced they should divorce.

At that moment the world he had created, believing it would be good for all of them, dissolved in less than ten minutes. He had never gotten over the fact that she had disregarded any and all of his feelings. Who in their right mind ended a three-year marriage without any explanation, then calmly returns to the kitchen to peel potatoes for dinner as though nothing had happened?

Days, weeks, months later, he tried not to hold Bridgett's decision against her. He knew better than anyone that sometimes no matter how hard a person tried, they couldn't force themselves to have feelings for someone that didn't exist. After Bridgett's sudden request for a divorce had stopped stinging, he realized the truth.

He had never been in love with her either. Yes, he loved her, and they had a child together—a child bonded a man and a woman together for life. But falling in love with Bridgett? That was another issue.

Now, his daughter stood here condemning him for not being around when she was growing up, and it more than shocked him. It hurt. *Boy, she was having a real field day with him today.*

Hopefully, she had gotten most of it out of her system and Travis prayed that the next few weeks passed quickly. He was not prepared for whatever she had in store for him nor was he up for the task.

He wished he had the power to travel back in time. Return with Liz to a happier moment in her life. The month before last, they spent a long weekend in New York. Everything had been great, or so he thought, after he flew Liz back to her mother's. They'd shared some laughs, she'd even laced her arm through his when they walked down Fifth Avenue taking in the decorated windows all ready for the upcoming holiday. He couldn't help wonder if she would ever be happy again.

He clenched his jaw and turned toward Cecile, who shrugged. Didn't she just tell him Liz wasn't herself and he shouldn't take anything personally? Man. He had to stay on his toes and not judge—at least for a while. He would also have to become a fast learner since the two of them would be headed to Pennsylvania and their new life together in a few hours.

Cecile leaned in to whisper, "She and Bridgett agreed a few weeks ago that it would be okay to call her mother by her first name."

Travis blew out a heavy sigh. Typical in the past, whenever he and Bridgett had disputed certain parenting tactics they talked it over and always came to a livable agreement. This call-me-by-my-first-name topic was one she'd neglected to fill him in on. He reminded himself once again, that his daughter was still in shock. Top that off with a large dose of guilt and this kid didn't know which way was up.

She was only fifteen. And even though Travis drew the line at his daughter calling him anything but Dad, disciplining her now was completely out of line. She wasn't herself. He would wait until she became normal again before he brought this subject up for discussion. He might not be Father Of The Year, but he had feelings, too.

"Is she all packed to leave?"

The moment he said it he wanted to smack himself. Liz hated being treated like a child and he should have asked her, whether she was ready, not Cecile.

Liz swung around to face him, lips pressed together

in a slight grimace. “I’m right here, you know.”

Travis nodded. “Of course you are.”

He was the adult, and he’d have to take the lead when it came to tamping down emotions. Right now, it wouldn’t do either of them any good to get upset over feelings neither one of them could control. He would be patient, loving, and attentive—he would be what his daughter needed him to be, a father who was there..

Chapter Four

Fists clenched, Liz stormed, "Stop referring to me as if I'm invisible. I would never do that to you."

No, she wouldn't. She'd have at him, like she was doing right now. And he'd let her get away with it, anything to help her vent her frustration and pain. God help him.

She counted off on her delicate fingers, "First I lose my mother. And now I'm supposed to lose my home, too? The home I grew up in? My school, my friends? What are you giving up? Nothing."

Travis cringed and held his tongue. They'd discussed this two weeks ago after Bridgett's funeral. His business needed him in Pennsylvania where he and Liz would start their new lives together. She'd seemed okay with his plans then. What the hell happened during that time to change her mind?

Liz stomped over to the sofa and slumped down into its thick, down-filled cushions. Her bottom lip quivered as she grabbed a pillow and hugged it to her chest fiddling with the fringe. "I don't want to leave; I want to stay with Aunt Cecile and Uncle Rick. Go to Pennsylvania without me."

He ached to hold her in his arms, take all of this pain away and bear this burden for her. But unfortunately she would have to go through this process in her own way, no matter how long it took. God how he wished Bridgett were here. So he could thank her, for all the patience, guidance, love, and dedication she had given Liz. She had been one hell of a mother.

But that wouldn't happen. The hourly phone conversations with Bridgett about Liz were over. He was on his own. He needed to think before he spoke. A problem he'd been unable to control for a long time. And sadly, he would be the first to admit that his knowledge of teenage girls was limited.

Narrow eyes and chin jutted forward, Liz looked all of three year's old. Back then, a kiss and a lollipop would have snapped her out of her bad mood. Somehow Travis figured those means of negotiation were off the table now. No. This time it was going to take more than a lollipop to heal his daughter's hurt.

He looked at Cecile for support; her response was to make shooing motions for him to move closer to Liz.

"Pennsylvania has great skiing conditions just like here in Illinois."

Okay, so that was a tiny lie. Some years, the snow at the Pennsylvania slopes was man-made. It all depended on what kind of winter they experienced. And for the past few years, the northeast had been having some very mild winters. But snow was snow, right? Who cared where it came from?

A painful lump lingered in Travis' throat. He swallowed hard. "There is also tubing and sledding."

"It doesn't have Aunt Cecile."

Okay, she had him there. But his hands were tied on the decision to move. He and his business partner, Rob, had discussed in great detail which one of them would focus their efforts on getting their most recent warehouse, twenty minutes from Golden, Pennsylvania, up and running this year.

With Rob's new baby on the way, and Liz having to move in with Travis, now seemed like as good a time as any for them to relocate. Besides, Golden, Pennsylvania, was Travis' hometown and nothing but happy memories filled him when he recalled his youth.

Liz needed stability and Travis knew if he moved back to his hometown, that's just what they'd find. New York City, his home for the past six years, was no place to raise a teenager. He and Rob had agreed Rob would stay in Long Island since that was where he and his wife had put down roots.

"I'll be relocating, too," he said after he sat beside her. "We can both start over."

Her glare cut right through him. "I didn't ask you to do that."

True. The school system in Golden was second to none, crime was virtually nonexistent, and the mountain air was clean and fresh. Who could want anything more? And although Travis had spent time and weighed the options before making his final decision to relocate, right now the move didn't seem as great an idea as he had originally thought.

Still, he couldn't help but think that the move to Golden would be good for Liz. If they stayed here she'd be reminded of her mother every minute of every day. In Golden, fresh surroundings might help her heal faster.

More than anything, he wanted to be there for her. Just like Bridgett had been. No matter how busy her day at the shop, Bridgett always went home to check on Liz after school. So Travis planned to rent an office somewhere in the center of town a short walk from the house he had fallen in love with. Was it so bad for him to want to provide his daughter with the support and love he knew she would need?

He tried again. “I found a house. It needs work, a lot of work actually, but it will be beautiful when we’re finished with the renovations.”

“Fine. You go spend time in your beautiful house.” She tossed the pillow aside and stared down at her long delicate fingers.

He reached over and touched her hand. To his surprise, she didn’t pull away. “You’ll love it, sweetie.” Liz had inherited many of her mom’s decorating talents such as mixing patterns and textures. She would love working on the house, she just needed to give it a chance. If only he could convince her. “It needs major renovations to get it the way we’ll want.”

Remaining mute, and clearly mutinous, she crossed her arms over her chest.

Cecile shot him a look that said, don’t give up.

“Come on, Liz. You love that stuff. Choosing fabric, carpet, and wallpaper.”

Not even a nibble.

Travis pushed on. “There’s so much to do in Golden. There’s an indoor and an outdoor ice-skating rink where all the kids hang out at after school and on weekends. There’s also an indoor arcade full of games and a bumper car track.”

The bumper car track was new, but Travis recalled skating at both ice-skating rinks when he was a teen.

The clock on the table changed hands and the crackle of the fire filled the void. He made one last attempt. “Oh, and a mall was built two years ago.”

Her head snapped up. “Can I walk to this mall?”

Bingo! "No, but I can drive you," he added quickly, hoping to keep up her somewhat excited attitude. "You get your driver's permit this year, don't you?"

She nodded slowly.

"Once you can drive on your own, you won't have to rely on me."

Still nothing. What teenager didn't look forward to driving?

"I thought you were excited about learning to drive?" He didn't care if she pretended not to need him. He knew better. Gently he moved her beautiful chin around until she was facing him.

Her small shoulders quivered. Tears streamed down her face. "Mom was teaching me—"

Liz folded into his arms and sobbed.

So that's why she was no longer excited to drive, and he didn't blame her one bit. "It's okay, honey."

Liz wiped at her eyes and pulled back. "I'm not a particularly good skier either."

Travis drew a deep breath. "What are you talking about? I've seen you ski. You do fine."

"I only do the bunny slopes."

He pulled a white handkerchief from his back pocket and handed it to her. "It doesn't matter. You'll improve once you start to ski every weekend, sometimes even after school."

Cecile walked over to Elizabeth and stood on the other side of her. Her voice was low and comforting as she reached out to touch Liz's shoulder. "Sweetie, we've talked about your moving to Golden to be with your father."

The teen stared up at the aunt she adored.

Cecile gently brushed Liz's bangs out of her eyes. "It will be fine, you'll see. And think of all the help he'll need fixing up the house. You have such good taste."

The teen sent her aunt an uneasy look.

Cecile continued, "You also have the wonderful ability to make friends fast. Why not go out for the tennis team next fall?"

Liz shrugged and blotted her eyes with the handkerchief.

"It certainly would be a shame to waste your talent."

Travis nodded. Liz had been one of the few freshmen to make the tennis team last fall and she loved the game. Quick to return the ball and faster to catch her opponent unawares, she won almost all her matches.

"You and your father should be together now. You need each other." Cecile squeezed Liz's shoulder gently and slipped out of the room.

The teen let out a long large sigh. Her shoulders softened as the fight in her slowly dissipated. Travis paced the small living room. He guessed it had to be tough having adults telling you what to do, especially when you wanted to grow up so fast.

He wouldn't know about that.

When Travis turned ten he got a job bagging groceries. Since he'd been too young for working papers he worked only for tips. He'd learned fast and hard the value of please, and thank you. On weekends he delivered newspapers on his bike. The paper distributor knew of his situation and had paid him cash each week. He had to. The year before, his father left

Travis' mother with nothing but a broken heart and a pile of bills. But his mom was a survivor and she never showed her pain. Still, he had sensed it.

During the day, his mother waited tables at a local diner; at night she took tickets at the only movie theatre in town. She had been a proud woman and Travis learned the value of a good work ethic from her. All those years it had been him and his mom so he had never really had a childhood like all the other kids.

While they were out playing stickball on the dead end street, waiting for their moms to call them in to eat dinner, he was already inside preparing dinner so his mother would come home to a hot meal at the end of her long day. His greatest happiness came from knowing he'd helped her and that together they had built a life to be proud of.

Travis wanted more for his daughter. He wanted her to have a normal life. To have the opportunity to be a kid and spend time with her friends enjoying her youth and not tied down to a job that aged her before it was necessary. Damn, life was too short.

Liz swallowed hard then turned to meet his gaze. "I feel so alone."

Travis sat beside her and guided his daughter's chin to face him again. "I'm here now, and you will never be alone again."

Her bottom lip quivered as fresh tears wet her cheeks. She curled into his arm and buried her face in his cotton pullover. Then his little girl sobbed harder.

Travis hugged her hard wishing he could take all her pain. "We're going to be all right, Liz, you'll see."

Now, if he could convince himself.

A few minutes later, Liz pulled out of Travis' arms.

"I'll get my coat."

"Okay." Travis watched Liz hurry upstairs then he stood and slipped into his own jacket. Cecile and Rick came into the hallway as he slung her duffel over his shoulder.

What did she have in this thing, bricks?

At the front door, Liz hugged Cecile. "Bye, Aunt Cecile, I love you."

Cecile returned the teen's hug. "Love you too, Button."

Liz stripped her gaze from her aunt and turned to kiss her uncle. Tears glistened in his daughter's eyes as she quickly hugged him. A moment later, she snatched her jacket and headed toward the rental car he left outside.

Travis shot a grateful look at Cecile and Rick. "Thanks for everything. You two really are the best."

Cecile hugged Travis warmly. "She's been a little touchy this week. Moving isn't sitting well with her. But you know how it is. She's young and fragile."

"I'll try to keep that in mind."

"And don't forget," Cecile continued, "she feels like her world has come to an end. That's natural. She'll be fine once she starts school and makes new friends. She had dozens of them here. Travis, don't worry. Liz is stronger than she lets anyone believe. Be patient."

He grinned at the petite, red-haired woman smiling up at him. A spray of freckles dotting her crinkled nose, warm and sincere, Cecile had been the first to welcome him into Bridgett's family years ago when he arrived in Chicago. Taking to her immediately, he'd been very grateful. From that day on, she'd remained his favorite of Bridgett's siblings.

"I know she'll miss you both."

Cecile's eyes filled with tears. Elizabeth had always been a large part of Cecile and Rick's life. They had helped Bridgett with shuffling Liz to and from school and tennis matches to picking up slack and driving car pools. They supported, cheered, and encouraged Liz in every endeavor.

Unable to have children, Cecile and Rick had always treated Liz like their own. Travis couldn't help feel that taking Liz away would no doubt be the cause of an even deeper void in Cecile's life. As if losing her sister and her best friend had not been enough for her to endure.

Quickly, Cecile stood on her tiptoes and kissed him on the cheek. She'd never been one for emotional greetings of any kind. Without another word, she slipped inside.

He reached out and shook Rick's hand. The older man's warm blue eyes and strong handshake said more than words ever could. Travis and Rick had spent countless Sunday afternoons watching football games and hanging out when Liz had been just an infant. Rick had been the type of person Travis had felt comfortable around from the get go. He'd always be grateful for his friendship.

"Call if you need us," Rick said.

Travis nodded. Cecile and Rick were good people with Liz's best interests at heart. He knew this wouldn't be the last he saw of them. Their bond with Liz was too strong. He hoped they'd visit. If not, he would make sure he and Liz got back out here to see them.

Travis headed toward the SUV where his daughter waited. He had never been more insecure of anything he was about to do. Hands tied, it was a change he had to make for both of them.

Outside, he saw Liz's head bobbing in time to the music. Her moods swung like a pendulum on a clock. He smiled and brushed all negative thoughts about Pennsylvania aside. Now that he was a full-time father, he had to believe in himself and his choices. If he didn't, who would?

When he climbed into the driver's seat the stereo blasted. *So this was her master plan? To blow out his eardrums?* He reached over and without thinking, turned the radio down.

She cocked her head and lifted a single eyebrow, appraising him. Then she reached into the back seat and rummaged through her duffel, pulling out her Ipod and earphones.

Good. Let her listen to that. As long as he didn't have to hear rap's top forty all the way to the airport, it was all good.

He backed the car out of the driveway and sensed the radio incident was only one small example of how his life would now become a series of struggles and compromises. He would have to pay close attention to his daughter over the next few weeks. He wanted nothing more than to get closer to her, understand what she needed and when. Question was—would she allow him that luxury?

Liz had been closer to Bridgett. After all, they lived together. Travis on the other hand, only saw Liz one or two weekends a month depending on her schedule. Juggling school, helping out at her mother's shop, and her tennis team responsibilities had to be hard. Especially since she played tennis all year in order to continue improving her skills.

Half an hour further up the road, Travis spotted a sign advertising a steak house off the next exit. Before asking whether Liz wanted to stop, he took the exit. A moment later remembering the incident at Cecile's too clearly, he covered his butt. "Want to grab dinner here before we head to the airport?"

He hated airline food and had skipped the meal on his flight in to Chicago. He also remembered Cecile saying Liz hadn't eaten today.

She pulled an earbud from her ear. "Whatever."

"What does that mean?"

She rolled her eyes and didn't answer.

Too bad teenagers didn't come with owners' manuals. At the restaurant, he climbed out of the SUV and slammed the door. Damn rain. It turned beautiful white snow into black slippery slush.

He walked around to Liz's door careful not to slosh too much muck around. She had worn those suede beige fuzzy boots and although he knew the weather would ruin them, he sure as hell didn't want to be the one who got blamed for it.

As the door swung open she jumped out.

Splat! Slush covered the bottom of his jeans. His mouth dropped open.

Liz looked up at him. "What?"

"I would have opened the door for you. Be careful, it's slippery." Oddly enough, her boots remained unscathed. He ignored the need to point that out.

She shook her head. "I'm not a baby. And you've got to be kidding about the door."

"No, I'm not kidding. It's what a gentleman does. He opens the car door, any door, for a lady."

"Well, I don't need *anyone* to do *anything* for me." She forced the zipper on her jacket up.

Travis tried again. "Someday you might like a guy to open a door for you."

"I don't think so." Her sarcasm cut through him.

They approached the restaurant and he reached for the doorknob a moment too soon then he probably should have given Liz's present attitude.

She stopped and clenched her jaw. With pursed lips, she tilted her head and studied him.

Travis retracted his hand. God, this child was stubborn. He stepped back and let her open the door by herself but waved one hand in a gesture of courtesy. "Ladies first."

Her gaze flicked upward and she stepped inside. Travis rubbed his brow.

Dear God, please give me the strength, patience, and whatever the hell else I need to get through the next few weeks.

A short while later, a waitress with the name Dot displayed on her tag, brought over his beer, and the soda Travis ordered for Liz when she'd slipped into the ladies room after they arrived. At least she had taken the Ipod ear buds out once they'd been seated. That meant something, right?

The waitress placed the drinks on their table and before walking away winked at Travis. Leave it to Liz not to miss a trick.

When the waitress was out of earshot, she snapped. "Do all women wink at you?"

Travis shrugged.

Elizabeth snorted. "Whatever."

"Liz, do you know any other word besides,

whatever? Because I'd bet money it drove your mother crazy, too."

His daughter glared at him. "I do *not* want to discuss my mother."

The pain in her eyes sliced through him. He should have known better than to mention Bridgett. It was too soon. "I'm sorry. I should have realized."

"Just forget it." She sank deeper into the worn red vinyl that lined their booth and crossed her arms defiantly. Then she wiped at her eye with the end of her sleeve that hung all the way down to her palm.

Travis cringed. He'd made her cry. Mental note: Do *not* do that again. He went back to reading the menu. "What are you going to have?"

"I'm not hungry."

"You could have something small."

"No, thank you."

Travis closed his menu. If she wouldn't eat, what was the point in staying? Besides, anything he did eat would only sit in his chest from aggravation. "We should leave."

"But you said you were hungry."

"I've changed my mind."

Travis pulled out his wallet and tossed a twenty onto the table. Maybe she'd want to eat later. He knew he would. "How about we grab a burger at the airport?" Swearing he saw his daughter's face brighten, he tilted his head and studied her closer.

"Really?"

"Sure." Right now, he'd eat anything, anywhere, as long as it made her happy.

Travis watched Liz bite her bottom lip, just like her mother used to. A shot of melancholy washed over him.

From that moment, he knew he'd do whatever it took to help his daughter through her grief.

She shot him an uneasy look. "Or maybe a salad—unless the waitress at the airport gapes at you, too."

Travis smiled. "I'm sorry she winked at me, okay? I'm sure she was just being friendly."

"Whatever." Liz kept her hands in her lap and played with her fingers.

Travis promised himself to learn to read her expressions better, her gestures too. She gave signs. Small and subtle, but they were there. Who knew a wink from a total stranger could get him into so much trouble?

When they approached the door to the restaurant, he stepped back and let Liz lead the way. If she wanted to open her own doors, so be it.

To his surprise, she rolled her eyes again. Apparently his attempt at pleasing her hadn't worked. No matter what he did, he just couldn't get this kid's approval. The optimist in him held out hope. Time had been known to change many things.

At the airport, Liz sat two seats away from Travis listening to her Ipod while they waited for their flight to be announced. Holiday music filtered through the speakers in between flights being announced. Sadness rippled through him. Usually he was in good spirit this time of year, but losing Bridgett had more than put a damper on any fast approaching holiday celebration. How in the hell would his daughter deal with Christmas this year? It had always been her favorite holiday.

The empty plastic container from the chicken Caesar salad she'd inhaled after they'd arrived at the airport sat next to her. Travis balled up the wrapper from his double cheeseburger and walked their trash to the nearest bin.

When he returned to their seats, Liz stifled a yawn and rubbed her eyes shadowed by dark circles.

Travis' chest tightened. He would have liked to sit closer so she could lean her head against his shoulder and take a nap. But even he knew not to suggest such a thing. Right now, she viewed him as the enemy who had taken her away from the only home she'd ever known, her friends, her family, and everything else she held near and dear.

That was okay. He'd give her as much time as she needed to come around. In the meantime, he'd be here for her. Travis stole a quick look.

"What?"

"You look just like—" As soon as he said it, he cursed himself. Idiot. "I'm sorry."

For the first time since he'd arrived, the corners of her mouth turned up. "Mom?"

He nodded.

"That's a compliment I can live with."

Well, what do you know?

The teenager glanced back down at the beige suede boots covering her tiny feet, and moved her head to the beat of the music coming from her Ipod.

She smiled.

And that was a great start.

Chapter Five

Saturday afternoon, Rebecca and her mother stood inside the entrance to Rosenblatt's Department Store as hordes of busy holiday shoppers pushed their way in and out of the store. What in the world had compelled *them* to come here on the weekend, especially during the Christmas season?

Seventy-five percent off, that's what!

Holiday music played in the background as Rebecca unbuttoned her winter jacket and pulled her favorite cashmere scarf from around her neck. "It's hot in here."

Leigh fanned herself. "Yes, it is."

They walked further inside the store where children screamed, babies cried, and sales clerks walked around, spritzing unsuspecting passersby with perfume. Luckily, Rebecca had dodged that bullet, the woman behind her, not so much. The short stout woman gasped for air and coughed as the saleswoman apologized tenfold.

They took the escalators up since the line for the elevators was packed with moms and strollers filled with loud, abrasive children.

"Is it just me?" Rebecca asked.

"No, sweetheart. I don't understand what's with some mothers. I always carried healthy snacks with us so when you became bored or hungry I could give you something to keep you busy."

They hopped off the escalators on the third floor, women's wear. Rebecca stood and surveyed the scene before her. Dozens of women rummaged through racks crammed with sale items. "Do I need a suit that badly?"

"At seventy-five percent off, I'm not letting you miss this." Leigh slipped one arm through Rebecca's to lead her into the area marked "business attire." Half an hour later they were both deep in the trenches of high-end discounted suits flying off the racks.

"How about this one?" Leigh's voice ramped up a notch in an effort to be heard. She held up a pin-striped navy blue suit.

Rebecca tentatively reached out and touched the fabric. "I don't think so. I was hoping for something brighter."

"Hmm. A *bright* business suit. Do they even make those?"

"I saw one in the circular. It was a beautiful midnight blue."

"Midnight blue? You mean like sapphire?" Leigh pulled a red sleeveless sheath from the dress rack behind her. Holding it out before her she ooohed and aaahed. It had a deep V neck and a slit that went all the way down to God knows where.

"Wow. That's quite a dress. Out to impress someone?" Rebecca asked.

Leigh looked hurt. "Sweetheart, I told you about Benjamin."

"Oh right, the guy you met on the cruise." Rebecca rifled through another section of suits.

Upbeat tone from a moment ago gone, her mother tossed the dress over one arm. "He's not *some guy*."

"Okay." Rebecca found a suit in a medium blue and tossed it over her own arm. "Then what is he?"

"Benjamin is the man who changed my life."

Rebecca stopped and studied her mother's stern expression. A store packed to the gills with shoppers was not the place for another sex talk. She walked to a rack a few feet away and pulled a dark purple suit, not the color she'd originally been shopping for, but beautiful nevertheless.

Leigh followed. "It's not blue. It's purple."

"I know, but I don't have anything like it."

"Try it on. It's a nice cut."

"Okay."

And with that the two women approached the fitting room and took their places on the long line.

"About Benjamin..." her mother began.

Rebecca didn't turn around but instead pretended not to hear, hoping she would take her disinterest as a hint and avoid all subjects pertaining to sex.

A voice boomed over the loudspeaker. "Sale in the men's department, eighty percent off sweaters will end in fifteen minutes."

To Rebecca's relief, three women bolted from the fitting room line. Head up, and alert for more defections among the ranks, she moved forward with the rest of the line.

"Rebecca."

"Yes?"

Frown lines creased her mother's forehead. "Benjamin and I are serious."

The woman was like a child with a one-track mind. "About what?" she murmured and opened her phone to check for messages.

The line moved; they shuffled forward. "About us. Will you put that thing away!"

Rebecca slipped the phone into her purse. "That's great, Mom."

"Good. Because I want you to like him."

"I'm sure I will," she rationalized. "You're a pretty good judge of people."

Leigh nodded. "Well, thank you."

The line moved, leaving only one woman in front of Rebecca. *Thank God.*

"Because he's coming to town this weekend."

"He lives close by?"

"Oh no. He's at least three hours away by car."

Eyes narrowed, Rebecca turned to study her mother's face. "Wait. He's driving three hours to see you?" A sly grin dressed her mother's face. "But he'll have to drive the three hours back in the dark."

"Don't be ridiculous. I wouldn't dream of letting him do any such thing."

"That's a relief." Rebecca chewed at her bottom lip. "Wait. How will he get home if he doesn't drive?"
"He's staying over."

Rebecca nodded and shifted her weight to her left foot. "I forget you have a guestroom."

"Sweetheart, you can be so naïve."

"What does...oh, I get it. He'll stay with you. Okay, no further information needed, Mom." *Please. Please no further information.*

Rebecca noticed the saleswoman emptying a vacant changing room. It was her turn next. *Come on, come on, let's go already.*

"I told him not to drive all this way, especially since he needs time and energy to tie up all those loose ends before he can move."

Rebecca's brow wrinkled. "Move? To Golden?"

"Really, sweetheart, sometimes you can be so thick."

"Thick about what?"

Her voice was low. "Men."

"I am not."

"Yes, you are."

Rebecca fanned herself. "How exactly am I thick?"

"Darling, Benjamin is moving here to Golden so we can be together."

"Well, that makes sense." She'd said they were serious and if they needed to see if this thing between them would last, him moving closer was wise. Better that than have either one of them driving all that distance once a week or so.

"Of course it does. He'll move in at the end of the month."

"He got an apartment already? Wow, he does move fast."

"Next," the salesgirl announced.

"In a manner of speaking."

Rebecca waited as the salesgirl gave her a small plastic hanger with the number two printed on it. "What does that mean?"

"Benjamin is moving in with me. Isn't that wonderful?"

"Next!"

Speechless, Rebecca walked into the empty dressing room, shut the door and sank onto the bench. *What the hell had just happened?* Her mother met a man one short week ago and now he was moving to Golden and they were going to live together?

Talk about spontaneous, talk about ridiculous, talk about crazy choices.

Jeez, if she'd been the one to act so blatantly irrational her mother would have protested rather loudly. With reversed roles, she was expected to sit back and just accept the outcome. Talk about a double standard.

She gazed at the suits hanging on the opposite wall, waiting for her to try them on. Groaning, she rubbed her temples. All enthusiasm to shop disappeared. *What is happening to my life?* First Travis shows up and throws her off balance, now her mother, the one person who had always used her common sense to guide her through life, was leaping into a relationship with a complete stranger.

"Sweetheart, come see this gorgeous dress," Leigh called from the dressing room next door.

Rebecca opened the door and watched her mother turn in front of the full-length mirror in the outer dressing room. A few customers as well as the salesgirl in charge of the dressing rooms ooohed and aaahed. When Leigh turned, Rebecca's breath caught in her chest. As if the plunging neckline wasn't revealing enough, the side slit went clear up her thigh, leaving very little to the imagination.

"This is sure to make Benjamin hot."

Other customers nodded, the salesgirl giggled and Rebecca would have sworn her mother purred.

At that comment, Rebecca took refuge back inside her small dressing room. Her own mother was turning into a hootchi kootchi momma right before her eyes.

Was there a full moon tonight?

****

Normally when a pilot announced that due to inclement weather, the plane would have to circle the airport, Travis grew impatient. Tonight, however, nothing could have made him happier. He glanced at his daughter who leaned against his shoulder, breathing slow and deep. He lifted the lightweight blanket provided by the airline and covered her.

After fighting exhaustion, it had taken Liz almost the entire flight to fall asleep. Hell, he'd circle for two hours if it meant she got the rest she needed. No matter how grown up she tried to be, she still appeared tiny and frail to him. Liz would always be the little girl who sat in his lap every night for the first three years of her life, begging for another bedtime story.

But just as Travis was beginning to learn, he had little or no control over factors that contributed to his daughter's moods, he also had no control over the weather. Twenty minutes later the pilot announced they had gotten the okay to land.

The plane's sporadic movement startled Liz and she sat up. Dazed, she quickly moved away from Travis and glanced out the 737's small window.

Already midnight by the time they arrived in Golden, he pulled into the garage then walked around to his daughter's side of the car. He hated waking her but knew she would be more comfortable in her own bed.

"Wake up, sleepyhead," he whispered, brushing the back of his hand lightly against her cheek. She looked like an angel.

"I'm awake," she grumbled. Travis waited as she slunk out of the SUV, a minute later following him into their house through the mudroom. He hoped she wasn't too tired to notice the work he'd done to her room.

Inside, Travis placed Liz's bags in the entrance foyer and flipped on the lights. She said she'd packed only what she absolutely had to have for the first week until Cecile sent the rest of her belongings. If that was true, why the hell were her bags so heavy?

Liz stretched.

He grabbed her suitcases and started up the long winding staircase that led to the second floor. Now he knew how mules felt when their owners loaded their backs with provisions.

Liz followed silently behind him.

Inside her room, Travis pivoted quickly so he wouldn't miss the expression on her face after she took it all in. "I did it myself in only a few days." He'd painted, moved in furniture and hung dainty white lace curtains. *It looked damn good if he did say so himself.*

"Thanks?"

His enthusiasm popped like a balloon hitting a sharp object. "Not the right color?"

Her mouth gaped. "It's a Pepto-Bismol nightmare."

Don't hold back kid. Tell me how you really feel. "You used to love pink."

She turned in a circle and studied the room. "When I was three."

He sighed. "We can have it repainted."

"When?"

"Soon." He scanned the room with his hands on his hips. White furniture, stuffed animals, ruffled curtains—what girl wouldn't love this? He sighed. *Okay, maybe it was a tad babyish.*

"I probably should have gotten professional help."

Liz looked at him with wide eyes. "Professional help?"

He nodded. "An interior designer. Someone who knows exactly what young women your age like."

"Nah. They would probably load it all up with flowers and fru fru. I can do it myself."

Travis angled her a glance. "You can sew?"

"What does that have to do with anything?"

Ahh, everything.

Liz blew out a deep breath. "I'll think about it."

"Okay."

His thoughts drifted to Becca. Maybe he could hire her to redo Liz's room and renovate the rest of the house. He reminded himself to be careful when he approached her. Running into her the other day had reminded him that they had unfinished business he needed to address if they were both going to live in the same town.

"Look, it's late. Let's get some sleep."

Liz grunted and dug through her duffel bag.

Travis closed her bedroom door and retreated to his own room. But sleep would not come. His mind raced. So Liz hadn't loved the color he's chose for her room. No big deal. It was just paint. And if a coat of paint was all it took to satisfy her, that was one easy out.

He folded his hands behind his head and glanced around the master bedroom. It was beige. Everything was beige. There was so much he wanted to do to this house like strip the moldings down to the original oak he knew lie underneath so many coats of dated paint, and refinish all the floors.

A smile crept onto his face as visions of Becca filled his mind. He knew she could be the answer to his renovation project. But he also knew having her around on a consistent basis might be something she wouldn't agree too. Especially since she made it clear she had no time for him.

He had no one to blame but himself for her chilly welcome. After all, he was the one who had screwed things up between them. Leaving school and following Bridgett home, marrying a woman he barely knew so his child would have a father. He had done all of that without ever contacting Becca. Sure she still resented him. Who could blame her?

Since his divorce Travis had had relationships with other women. But none of them lasted. There was only one woman he had longed for time after time, year after year. Becca. Now that life had brought him back to Golden, it was time to face the past and make amends. He needed her in his life. Knowing Becca, groveling of some kind would be involved.

Tomorrow morning he would stop in at Designs of Distinction. Winning her trust back might be hard, but he'd had endured harder. Like moving to Chicago with Bridgett after they'd discovered she was pregnant—and leaving Becca behind.

Believe it or not, Travis had good intentions back then. He hoped that given time, Becca would forget him and get on with her life. She deserved a man who didn't leave abruptly without an explanation—a man who would stay by her side no matter what, a man who would love her like she deserved and nothing less.

Laying here now, he wondered if she would agree to work with him on his renovation project or tell him to find someone else. He figured if she gave him a hard time he still held an ace that just might persuade her to reconsider.

Liz—the teenager whose eyes could melt the

coldest person's heart.

And even though Travis didn't like to play dirty, he had to admit asking for Becca's help with Liz's bedroom would be the perfect way to break the ice.

****

Bright and early the next morning, Liz padded into the kitchen in her pajamas, rubbing both hands up and down her arms.

"Morning, sleepy head."

She scowled. "It's cold in here."

Travis leaned against the old Formica kitchen counter top reading the morning newspaper. "Didn't you pack a robe?"

She yawned. "Can't find it."

He tossed her his navy blue terry cloth robe from the back of his stool.

"Aren't *you* cold?"

"Nah." He never felt the cold. Sweatpants and a t-shirt were more than enough for him. He'd grabbed his robe on instinct this morning when he remembered Liz was with him. She skillfully caught the ball of blue terry cloth before it hit the dated black and white linoleum floor.

She studied it for a moment then asked. "What am I supposed to do with this?"

"You could put it on. You said you were cold."

She held the robe in front of her like it was a diseased animal and shook her head. "I don't think so."

Travis filled his coffee mug and watched her read the label on the inside of his bathrobe and whistle at the brand name. "So maybe you're not a *totally* bad dresser."

Teenagers and status. He'd have to remember how

closely the two went hand-in-hand.

Liz slipped her arms into his robe. It was two sizes too big for her. Travis smiled as she rolled up the sleeves countless times before reaching for the container of orange juice on the kitchen table.

"Aroma from my dee-licious pancakes wake you?"

She rolled her eyes at his attempt at humor. "You made pancakes?" Her voice was laced with sarcasm.

Two could play at this game. He shot her a wide smile and walked over to the kitchen table. "Ha ha." Then he reached for the covered plate he had placed the pancakes on to keep them warm and pretended he was going to remove it. "Well, if you don't want any."

"Hey," she squawked, smacking his hand back.

He retracted his hand and chuckled. Thank God she was hungry, and...what do you know, she even laughed.

She piled a stack of pancakes, tall enough to feed the NFL onto her plate, and proceeded to slather them with butter and syrup.

Travis sipped his coffee. "By the way, we need to do some serious grocery shopping. You start school in a few days and our refrigerator is bare. I figured we could go together and fill it up

"Don't remind me."

"About school or grocery shopping?"

She cut into her pancakes with her fork ignoring his comment. "Umm. Pancakes are good."

Travis sipped his coffee and smiled. "Yes, pancakes are good, but we need other food."

"Mom did all the shopping."

"Liz, please."

She put her fork down and drained half a glass of orange juice.

"I have no idea what you like. Come grocery shopping with me."

She frowned.

"It won't be that bad." He sighed. Jeez to get her to do anything was like pulling teeth.

What happened to the good old days when she used to love going places with him? Accompanying him around town in his truck while he ran errands. Had it really been that long since he had been the most important man in his daughter's life?

Liz studied his face. "Okay."

He walked to the kitchen sink and deposited his coffee mug making a mental note that when they renovated the kitchen and installed a dishwasher he would have to make sure it was fronted with the same cabinetry they chose for the rest of the room. Dishwashers didn't exist in the early 1900's and he wasn't about to blow the home's authenticity. Covering the front would be the perfect camouflage because he wasn't about to start washing dishes anytime soon.

"I'm going upstairs to shower. Finish eating. We leave in thirty minutes." He turned toward the stairs.

"No. Can. Do."

He stopped in his tracks. "Why?"

"I need a shower, too."

He looked at her. "Right." She probably doesn't take bubble baths and wash her hair at night anymore either. Why hadn't that occurred to him? More importantly, how long would it take him to stop treating her as if she was three? "How much time do you need?"

"I don't know. Half an hour? The sooner you get out, the sooner I can get in."

"Okay. We leave in one hour." Sharing a bathroom

was going to be tough. He'd always had his own. He made a mental note to add one onto his bedroom and another powder room downstairs.

He hesitated before asking the next question. He wasn't sure how to say it, how she would interpret it, but it had to be addressed so he figured he should just wing it. "About Christmas—"

Liz got a far away look on her face. "Mom loved decorating the tree."

He wasn't ready for her honest reply.

And even though her eyes were teary, she stayed strong. "Aunt Cecile is sending all the boxes with the ornaments Mom and I collected over the years."

"Liz, if this is too much for you—"

"No. I want to do it. It was a yearly tradition for us." She muttered, "Mom would want me to. But not today, okay? Can we do the tree thing next week? I mean the ornaments won't be here until then anyway."

Travis nodded. That had gone smoothly. He hoped the rest of the day continued the same way.

Chapter Six

After showering and changing into clean clothes, Travis knocked on Liz's bedroom door. "Are you almost ready?"

"I can't find my toothbrush."

He could barely hear her above the loud music permeating the door. "May I come in?"

"Whatever!"

Travis opened her bedroom door and blew out a deep breath. *Had a bomb hit the room?* There were piles of clothes strewn about, along side the hangers all over the floor, the bed, everywhere.

He pointed to the radio and she hit the off button. "Can I ask a question?"

She rummaged through an overstuffed make-up bag and rolled her eyes. "You're going to anyway."

"Why are your clothes all over the place?"

"Nothing stays on those stupid satin hangers I found in the closet."

Another little something he had purchased thinking she'd like them.

Clearly frustrated, she collapsed onto the twin-sized bed. Pink and white pillows popped onto the already overflowing floor. "I can *not* go out without brushing my teeth. It's disgusting!"

He returned with a new toothbrush and an arm full of heavy-duty plastic hangers. "From the hall closet."

A smile blossomed over Liz's face.

Why couldn't she do that more often? This kid went from hot to cold faster than his kitchen faucet.

****

Later that morning in the parking lot at the Bag and Save, Travis listened as Liz read aloud from a brochure she had picked up at the courtesy counter about internet grocery shopping. Hell. Anything that prevented him from revisiting the inside of that madhouse again had to be a good idea.

Who knew little old ladies could be so vicious?

His ankle still throbbed from nearly being plowed down in the cereal aisle by a woman with a cane. God, she could move fast.

When he'd reached for the last box of oatmeal on the shelf all havoc broke out. Anger seethed from the elderly woman's eyes. She'd smacked him with her cane and barked, "Young man, you will not screw with my digestive system." He immediately backed down leaving the last box to her and told himself he didn't like oatmeal all that much.

Loading the bags into the back of their SUV, he couldn't believe he had needed two carts to wheel them outside. Sure, they had come here to stock their refrigerator, but he hadn't realized it would take eighteen grocery bags to accomplish. In every aisle, Liz repeated the same mantra, you have no good food to eat, and tossed items into the cart.

No kidding. He bit his lip wanting to remind her that he had been the guy who had supplied her with those delicious pancakes this morning, but decided against it.

He had to admit, he was more than glad to see her

appetite return and wasn't about to debate her menu choices. As a grown man he tended to steer away from carbs. But Liz was a teenager with five times his metabolism. If she wanted pasta, she could have pasta. At least she had chosen whole-wheat penne. There would be plenty of time later for a talk on the importance of vegetables in her diet.

They slid into the car and fastened their seatbelts.

"The computer in my office is all hooked up and working. Go on-line and set up an account for us. Do whatever's necessary to get us registered. This whole Internet shopping thing sounds like the perfect solution for us."

"I guess so."

"Before I forget, the laundry gets picked up on Tuesdays and is dropped off on Thursdays."

Liz frowned. "I do *not* want some stranger washing my underwear. I'll take care of my own laundry, thank you very much." Her voice cracked. She turned and gazed out the car window.

A light snow began to fall. Travis watched her wrap her arms around herself. He cranked up the heater.

Looking at her sitting next to him with her arms crossed stubbornly across her chest, he wanted nothing more than to pull her into his arms and hold her. But his daughter's chin, jutted forward in an independent stance, told him now wasn't the time. He sighed. Sometimes she tried too hard to be strong, when would she see he was here for her?

"I understand. I have always had someone do my laundry. I never seem to have the time. But if you prefer to take care of your own, that's fine."

She continued to stare out the window.

He should have stopped when he was ahead. But he was so proud of her attempt to take care of herself; he couldn't help it when the words flew from his tongue. "Your mom would be very proud of you."

His daughter's head spun to face him. "You know *nothing* about my mother."

His stomach knotted. Where had that come from?

"I don't think we should discuss this now." He turned his car slowly into traffic not sure what to expect next. All he wanted was to get home, on common ground, and forget about the stupid remark he just made.

Suddenly she screamed, "You left us!"

Travis swallowed hard. He made a left at the next corner. "Let's go home."

"My *home* is in Illinois."

Pulling into their driveway, Travis could swear he heard her whisper, "I hate you."

Inside Liz made a beeline for her room. Travis didn't even try and stop her. He was still reeling from the confrontation that had just taken place in the car. What the hell happened? A few minutes ago they were discussing groceries and laundry. How in the world had everything turned so bad so fast? Travis reminded himself to think before he spoke in the future.

Liz slammed her bedroom door. Travis cringed at the vibration. Holding a grocery bag tightly in his arms he thought he might crush its contents so he quickly placed it on the kitchen table. Fine. Let her have some time to herself. Mull things over. And first thing tomorrow he'd head over to Rebecca's store and ask for help, hell he'd beg if he had to. He'd do anything to get her to work with Liz on her bedroom and him on the rest of the house. In the meantime he'd put the groceries away, turn on the basketball game, and bask in the sanity of a cold beer.

****

That evening Michelle dropped by Rebecca's for a few minutes to help decide which suit Rebecca should keep. Thanks to her mother dropping the bomb that Benjamin was moving in with her at Rosenblatt's earlier, Rebecca hadn't even tried on the suits she'd chosen. She bought both and decided to return one. Now she couldn't decide which one.

The doorbell rang and Sherlock snapped to attention. The dog bolted barking from his plaid dog bed in the corner of the living room and jumped up and down in front of the door. His small tail spun round and round.

Rebecca opened the door, and Sherlock jumped in circles like a circus dog vying for Michelle's attention. Her friend bent and scooped him into her arms. He squirmed and licked her chin repeatedly.

Michelle placed the dog on the floor, then pulled a small soft hedgehog from her coat pocket.

Sherlock's ears perked. He jumped against her leg over and over.

She ripped the price tag off the toy and tossed it toward the basket already overflowing with toys. Sherlock scrambled over to get his new toy and settled down for a good chew.

Rebecca closed the door. "You spoil him."

"Right. And that basket full of toys just appeared one day?"

Rebecca shrugged. "You got me."

She rubbed her hands briskly. "Let's see this suit."

"Wine?" Rebecca lifted the bottle and filled her own glass.

"Always." Michelle reached over and helped herself.

"How'd the shopping go with your mom?" Michelle sipped her wine. "This is yummy."

"Well, it went." Rebecca walked into her bedroom with Michelle right behind her.

"What does that mean?"

Rebecca turned and sat on the upholstered bench at the foot of her bed. "She's in love and he's moving in. Just like that." She took a long pull of wine.

Michelle sat on the bed. "More details, please."

Rebecca filled her in about Mom and Benjamin.

"Good for her."

Rebecca's shoulders slumped. "Is there some contagious illness going around I don't know about?"

"Huh?"

All the wine in the world wouldn't relax her now. "Am I the only one who thinks she's jumping before thinking this through clearly?"

"She's a big girl, Beck."

"No shit. Thanks, because I wouldn't have seen that one on my own."

"Why are you so angry?" Michelle placed her wine glass on the nightstand, then turned to view her friend closer.

Rebecca stopped pacing. "I am, aren't I?"

Michelle nodded. "A little."

"I'm acting like a spoiled child. I should be happy for her but..."

"You don't want her to be taken advantage of."

Rebecca ran her fingers through her untamed hair.

"You read about these guys who find vulnerable widows and drain their bank accounts. It's scary." She drained her wine glass.

"You do hear about that happening quite a bit, but don't forget, your mom is far from stupid and she enjoyed almost thirty years of blissful marriage with your dad. She knows what love is and whether it's real."

"Come on, Chelle, falling in love in one week? Seven days? That's a tough pill to swallow."

"I don't know, I've heard it happens."

Rebecca blew out a long sigh. "She's asked me to meet them for drinks."

"Good. Go. Meet him. See what he's like."

Rebecca nodded.

"He could be a really nice man, Becc. Maybe someone just like your dad."

"I hardly think so, he was..."

"Special. I know. But give your mom the benefit of the doubt. Aren't you always saying what a good judge of a person's character she is?"

"Yes. I am." She slipped into the suit pants and zipped them.

"That color is beautiful." Michelle walked over to the full-length mirror in Rebecca's bedroom to gain a better view. "These are gabardine, they'll last you forever."

Rebecca nodded, then buttoned the midnight blue blazer. "It is a beautiful color, isn't it?"

"It's also a perfect fit. You should keep it. I wouldn't even try on the purple. This is the one."

She turned and faced Michelle. "Thanks."

A large smile covered her friend's face. "No

problem. Although I'd love to stay, drink wine, and hear more about your mother's sexual exploits, I've got to go. Chris and I are having dinner with his boss and his wife." She rolled her eyes. "Now that woman could take a lesson or two from your mother."

They walked back into the living room.

"How so?" Rebecca asked.

Sherlock ran over, and Rebecca picked him up so he wouldn't trip Michelle on her way out.

"She's so rigid. God, they're married, but I don't think they have sex."

Rebecca burst into laughter. "Tell me how you really feel, Chelle."

"Seriously." Michelle buttoned her coat. "Getting laid would do her a boatload of good." She patted Sherlock's head and headed down the stairs that led to the street. "Still on for dinner, tomorrow night?"

"Absolutely."

"Okay, thanks for the wine."

Rebecca locked the door and placed Sherlock on the floor. He raced back over to his toys.

A sense of satisfaction skittered through her as she changed from her new suit into comfy sweats and a T-shirt. Michelle had a point. Her mother was a very good judge of people and Rebecca was probably worried about nothing; still, she would feel better after she met this Benjamin in person.

****

Monday morning found Travis at Designs of Distinction. While Becca talked with a client on the telephone, he leaned against an antique oak armoire and waited for her to finish. He needed to talk to her about his renovation project. More importantly, he needed to discuss the past, their past. Perhaps if she knew the reason why he did what he did back then, she'd be more understanding.

With one glance around the shop, it occurred to him why she had been able to run a successful business for the past ten years. She had good taste.

Everything in the shop, from an antique cherry sideboard displaying a silk floral arrangement in a clear vase filled with marbles, to the upholstered furniture and window treatments carefully placed throughout, had been impeccably planned, chosen, and displayed. There wasn't one thing Travis saw that he didn't like. Even though he and Bridgett had only been married three years, she was always tuned into the latest home design shows on television, and he'd be the first to admit that as a man, he knew way too much about home design.

While Becca spoke to a client about fabric for throw pillows and ordering additional furniture, Travis eyes skimmed over her form. She'd not aged one bit and still looked as young and vibrant as she had in high school. That first morning, stopping to inquire if a stranded woman needed help, nothing could have prepared him for their meeting. He had no idea she chose to stay in Golden. But he was glad she had.

He also hadn't been prepared for his body's reaction to her. How the muscles in his stomach contracted in surprise and his groin tightened in delight. But then, she had always had that effect on him. Looking at her now, he realized just how much he had missed her all these years. And what a fool he had been not to come home sooner.

"Yes, Mrs. Lawrence, the fabric we chose for your

family room will work wonderfully with your antique mahogany pieces. No. I don't mind adding three more throw pillows to your order. They will, of course, arrive a little later than the rest of your merchandise. Yes. I'll let you know when they come in." She placed the receiver back in its charger.

When Travis cleared his throat, and she jumped, he stepped closer. "Sorry, I didn't mean to scare you."

Rebecca rummaged through some files on her desk. "How long were you standing there, eavesdropping?"

"I didn't mean to. I mean—I wasn't. You were on the phone when I came in. I waited for you to finish."

She stood and walked to the file cabinet behind her desk. When she bent to replace a folder, Travis couldn't help but appreciate her curvaceous bottom and tiny waist.

She turned and caught him staring. His cheeks flushed. "What can I do for you?" She pushed her hair back off her shoulders, a habit she had for as long as he could remember. Instantly he knew he was home again.

Travis sat in the chair next to her desk and spread his long legs out, then placed both hands behind his head. He tried to read her face but could not. Although he knew her better than anyone when they were younger, the expression Becca wore now was foreign to him.

He kept his voice low. "Remember I told you I'm relocating to Golden?"

****

Rebecca swallowed hard and walked to the front of her desk. How could she forget? Especially when he showed up unannounced and reminded her?

"I need your help with a house I've purchased. It needs extensive work." He rubbed his hands together. "However, before we discuss business, I think it is more important to discuss our past."

Rebecca wanted to shout, *No, it's not necessary*, but when their eyes met, his looked so sad, she couldn't bring herself to stop him.

Besides, wanting to talk about their past was very mature and she hadn't given him credit for having come that far. After fifteen years, she was sure there was nothing Travis could tell her now that she needed to guard herself from. He could not hurt her anymore.

"I'm sorry."

Two little words that meant so much. Rebecca swallowed. Her mouth dried. His voice was low. She swore remorse emanated from his eyes.

"I didn't contact you because I was ashamed of myself. Immature and afraid that I'd hurt you and not knowing what I could say to make you feel better only made it harder for me."

"So you quit school and disappeared."

He ran his hand through his already mussed hair. She could see this was hard for him, but she wanted answers.

"I moved to Chicago with Bridgett to be closer to her family. I got her pregnant in college. We both quit school to raise our baby together."

Rebecca's breath caught in her throat. *He has a child. No. He couldn't have, wouldn't have.*

"It was after I first went to school. You know, when we agreed to see other people?"

She nodded. Only she had never seen anyone else. There hadn't ever been anyone else, until Mike.

"I still felt it was necessary to talk face-to-face."

She nodded over the lump forming in her throat. In all honesty, what had happened to him could have happened to anybody. "As for your apology and honesty, I thank you. Better late than never, isn't that what they say?"

Travis stood to stretch his legs.

"More coffee?"

"Okay." He walked to the coffee machine and filled two cups, added creamer, sweetener, and stirred. He placed her cup in front of her.

He lifted his cup for a toast. "To making amends and to the future."

Rebecca smiled and lifted her cup. "Here, here." She sipped the liquid and took comfort in its warmth.

Travis placed his cup on the end of Rebecca's desk and picked up the picture frame she'd kept there for years. "You have a beautiful family."

His eyes were full of sincerity and she wanted to agree with him and say, I know, but couldn't.

"Is something wrong?"

"No. Not at all." She forced a smile. "That's Mike and Annie. They were...well, I lost them in a car accident eight years ago."

Travis' eyes bulged. "I'm so sorry."

Rebecca shrugged. "Life isn't always fair." And quickly changed the subject. "You never did tell me what brought you back to Golden."

"I wanted my daughter, Liz, to have stability." He glanced out the large display window at the front of the store. "I have good memories from growing up here."

They were both quiet for a moment.

"Anyway, I relocated my daughter and my

"She and I, we met at a frat party and it—"

She put her hand up to stop him. "Too much information."

"Point is, I made some bad decisions. I didn't call you to explain and you deserved that much. You were hurt because of my insensitivity. I can't apologize enough." He lifted his eyes to meet hers. "You know, I loved you very much."

Rebecca cleared her throat. *She'd loved him more.*

"I don't expect you to welcome me back with open arms. What I did was wrong and I'll always be sorry for leaving. But I couldn't allow my child to be born without a father. I just couldn't."

Rebecca nodded. She knew all about how Travis' father had deserted him and his mother and how much Travis had resented him for it.

Not knowing what to say, she remained quiet. The last thing she expected was to feel sorry for him.

"I don't expect us to be best friends. But I would like us to get along."

"Travis. I know everyone in town. I'm proud of the business I own and it consumes most of my time. The last thing I have time for is a teenage grudge."

He blew out a deep breath of relief.

"What did you think? I'd get my gun and run you out of town?"

A wide grin covered his mouth. "No. You don't have a hurtful bone in your body."

She leaned on her desk and looked him in the eyes. "I'd be lying if I said I wasn't hurt them. We were kids who made promises. Disappointment isn't easy for a teenager to deal with. But we're adults now. I've moved on."

business here." Travis stood and paced. "Her mother died in a car accident a little over two weeks ago."

"I'm sorry." Rebecca's heart immediately went out to the young girl. She couldn't imagine what it must feel like to be so young and forced to deal with such a life-changing loss. Here she was a grown woman, who knew dealing with her own loss was difficult.

"Bridgett, Liz's mother, and I divorced twelve years ago."

The sadness Rebecca felt a moment ago disappeared. *He'd remained single all these years?*

"When I knew my daughter would be living with me full-time, I bought an old Victorian off Main Street, painted her room and moved in some furniture."

She bit her lip. "That was nice."

He hesitated. "I thought so, too." He shook his head. "What compelled me to think I'd know what a teenager likes, I haven't a clue. She hates it."

"Sounds to me like you had good intentions."

He shook his head. "I had no idea teenage girls were so moody." Travis studied his hands. "This morning I found her sleeping on the floor in the family room. Apparently she more than hates the color I painted her room. She detests her furniture as well."

"What color *did* you paint it?"

"Pink."

Her brow wrinkled.

"Pepto-Bismol pink, as Liz describes it."

Rebecca couldn't have hid the humor of the situation even if she wanted to. A roar of laughter escaped her throat.

"Yes, she thought it was funny, too. Bottom line is I want her to love her new room. To come home and want to spend time there."

Rebecca's back stiffened. She would have liked nothing more than to go home to a house where someone, besides Sherlock, waited for her. But some people were meant to live solitary lives. Weren't they?

"I know her bedroom needs repainting and redecorating. Come to think of it, the whole house needs major renovations."

"Wait a minute, did you buy the green Victorian on Main Street?"

Travis nodded.

"I heard it sold. It's a beautiful old house."

She had always loved that place. Its previous owner died and although it had been on the market for a long time, no one seemed to have the desire to renovate it to its original beauty. Her stomach flipped. For years she'd yearned for the opportunity to get inside and work on it.

"It's got a lot of potential."

"It sure does."

She recalled walking through it when the local Realtor held an open house not too long after the original owner passed away. Beautiful pumpkin pine floors yearned to be sanded and refinished. Thick molding needed to be stripped and stained. Nine foot ceilings dressed the first floor with a gorgeous coffered ceiling in the dining room with tin inserts that only needed polish. The old house had character, and endless possibilities.

"Done the right way, it could be returned to the beauty it once was. In my heart Liz will always be my little girl. Apparently I went overboard with my ideas."

"That's understandable."

And impressive—because before now, Rebecca didn't think it would ever be possible for Travis to put someone else before himself.

"It is?"

She nodded. "You were just doing something you thought she'd like. You got caught up in the moment."

"Right." He smiled. "Anyway, I hoped you could help me out."

Rebecca swallowed. *Help him out?*

"With the repainting of Liz's room for starters."

Painting. Sure, she could help him with that. Rebecca reached into her Rolodex and pulled out a business card. She didn't usually give out the phone numbers of independent contractors, but this was an exception.

Elizabeth shouldn't be punished because her father made poor choices when decorating her room, even if it had been done with good intentions. "This is the number of my most reliable painter. I'm not making any guarantees, but he might be available if you call him right away."

Travis sat straight up in his chair. "Really?"

"He's expensive," she warned.

"I don't care."

"Call and see if he's free. Tell him I referred you."

He smiled. "Thanks, Becca. I appreciate it."

"As far as her sleeping on the floor, I suggest you upgrade her bed to a full size, maybe even a queen—if her room is large enough."

"It is."

"Great. I've discovered teenage girls like a bigger bed than the standard twin. You can order everything you need from the furniture store off Main Street. In some cases they have been able to deliver the same day."

Travis blew out a deep breath. "Sounds great, I wish I could get right on it." His brown eyes penetrated hers. "Look I'm just going to come out and ask. Can you help Liz redecorate her room, then work on renovating the rest of the old beauty? Even though I've begun to strip the pine floors, I think I'm in over my head. I forgot how time consuming renovating an old house can be. It's been decades since I did that type of work." He ran the fingers of one hand through his hair.

"You started stripping the flooring?"

"Yes. Shouldn't I have?"

"Oh yes, of course. Those floors are beautiful."

"After I made such a big mistake in her room, I wouldn't even know what to recommend."

Rebecca softened. He seemed to be trying very hard to be the best father he could, and wasn't that what all good parents strived for?

"Since moving my business here," he went on, "I won't have time to get involved in the redesign. It's almost like I'm starting all over again. A few of my employees chose to make the move with me, but I need to hire more so I'll be tied up with interviews. Consulting on colors for the house will be all I have time for. And based on what I see here, I trust your judgment."

She nodded and hid the grin threatening to cover her lips. He would be too busy to do anything but approve colors? *Oh, this was better than good.* She could work on the old Victorian and at the same time, not have to interact with him. Yes!

His honesty, as well as the apology, demolished the

wall she'd built in his name years ago, but the attraction they'd shared was still strong. So strong it scared her. It would be easy to fall back into love with him, easy to forget their years apart.

But she had promised herself not to let him close to her. And that's why working on this project when he wasn't around, seemed perfect. She cast a glance at the appointment calendar she kept on her desk.

When she hesitated he added, "It's beige. The entire house, it's cold, empty. I'd like to see it with more color. You know, to bring out the character of the rooms? Warm them up and make them more inviting. I want Liz to love her new home." His voice was full of sincerity. "Did I mention it's beige?"

Rebecca couldn't help smile at his attempt at humor. She was also impressed. Most men were afraid of color and liked beige everywhere. Perhaps it could be fun working on the old house. And although her better judgment told her not to get involved with Travis' project, she couldn't help herself. The chance to dig her teeth into a project she'd secretly yearned for all these years, seemed too good to be true.

Besides, she wasn't doing this for him, she was doing it for his teenage daughter. And right now, helping this young girl felt like the right thing to do.

"Late next week I have an opening." She glanced at her watch. She also had an important appointment across town in less than twenty minutes. Mrs. Brady was interested in draperies.

"Why don't you have Liz stop in after school next week? Say Thursday about three o'clock?"

Her legs weakened from his warm smile. And when he leaned over and kissed her on the cheek, her entire body tingled. Staying uninvolved was going to be hard if he kept taking liberties like this.

"I can't thank you enough. You have no idea how much this means to me." He shook his head. "I mean to Liz."

Rebecca grasped the arms of her chair. Her heart beat crazily in her chest. She avoided his eyes. Until today, she had forgotten just how powerful his eyes could be—how her old feelings for Travis weren't buried as deeply as she hoped, and how all those feelings could be summoned back with just one of his irresistible smiles.

"Is there anything I need to sign? A contract?"

She shook her head. "Not right now. Let me meet with Elizabeth first. You and I can talk about the rest of the project at a later date. I can have a messenger deliver the contract to you. All you need to do to get this job started is sign and write out a check for a deposit."

"Great."

He stood so close she could smell his cologne and the mint he must have had before he entered the shop. She stood and he ran his index finger down her arm. Instinctively she pushed the chair back with her leg.

"If that's all."

Travis nodded and she used all her energy to usher him to the door. After she bid him goodbye, she closed the shop's door securely behind him and blew out a deep sigh of relief.

Accepting the task of redecorating Elizabeth's bedroom was one thing. Interfacing with a teenager wasn't anything new. She'd helped dozens of client's sons and daughters decorate their bedrooms over the past few years. But working with Travis on his renovation—that's where this agreement got sticky.

Instead of concentrating on what could and might backfire, she forced herself to come up with positive reasons this renovation project could be a good endeavor for Designs of Distinction.

For one, renovating the Victorian wouldn't just be good for her business; it might also be the jolt in the arm Golden's historic homes/real estate market desperately needed. People were opting to build new homes in the area rather than renovate the older ones, and it was truly a shame.

Perhaps if she helped Travis transform his home, people would take notice. And, in her own way, she might have a positive influence on the local real estate market, helping sales on the older homes to increase.

Absolutely, Rebecca assured herself, renovating Travis' house was a win-win for everyone. Travis was her employer. And their relationship purely a professional one.

Chapter Seven

Monday evening Rebecca met Michelle for their weekly dinner at Lucky Leo's, a restaurant/bar in Golden that always drew a crowd of people their age. The two women had been meeting here once a week for years ever since they both decided to stay in Golden and launch their careers. This was their time—to catch up and just enjoy each other's company and Rebecca looked forward to it every week.

Mondays were karaoke night, and although no one ever sung a good rendition of any song, it was still worth coming in just for the dollar margaritas served in huge goblets. And every once in a while there would be a really nice piece of eye candy at the bar they could both innocently ogle while enjoying their drinks and appetizers. After all, a little harmless man-watching didn't hurt anyone.

As usual the music from the karaoke machine blared throughout the bar. Rebecca worked her way through a group of women apparently celebrating a bachelorette night, dressed in skimpy skirts and midriff tops, hooting and hollering. They were already half-baked, and it was only seven o'clock. Then she passed a balding oriental man at the microphone, singing a very bad rendition of "I Got Friends in Low Places."

Finally, Rebecca saw Michelle at their usual table toward the rear of the restaurant, but she wasn't alone.

She squinted, but the lighting had been lowered because of karaoke night and she couldn't see squat. As she drew nearer, Michelle flashed a wide smile her way and the blond-haired man also turned to face her.

When she reached the table, Michelle introduced them. "Rebecca Evans, meet Kyle Wilson. Kyle, this is Rebecca."

He extended his hand. Rebecca returned his handshake and nodded. His hand was twice the size of hers, his handshake strong and solid. He was about six foot four, with blue eyes a person could swim in, and a deep dimple on his left cheek. When he smiled his perfect teeth almost gleamed at her. *He had to have had those whitened.*

A man across the room hollered and Kyle motioned he'd be right there. "I'm going to get another beer. But I'll be back." He winked at Rebecca and walked toward the bar.

"Well, what do you think?" Michelle asked.

"About what?"

"He's yummy."

Rebecca shrugged. "I don't like guys who wink. You can't trust them."

Michelle's mouth dropped open. "You never like anyone I set you up with."

"Set me up? You're trying to set us up?" Rebecca placed her coat on the hook just outside the booth then slid in opposite her friend.

"He's got quite a package. Watch when he comes back, those jeans fit him perrrrfectly."

"I think we should cancel tonight and you should go home to Chris and get laid. Because you are one horny s.o.b."

"I'm married. I can have sex anytime I want."

"Thanks for rubbing that in. As for Mr. Dimples over there, you can tell him no, thank you."

"Why? What would it hurt? Have a drink with him, get to know him better."

"I'm not interested in a one-night stand."

"What makes you think Kyle is?"

Rebecca nodded toward the bar where Kyle presently leaned one arm against the wall and seemed to be in a deep discussion with a redhead whose size thirty-eight D's had all his attention.

"He seems like just my type. All brawn and no brains."

Michelle rolled her eyes. "Fine. He's not the one, but trust me, a roll in the hay is just what you need."

Why is everyone so interested in me getting some sex? "I vote we change the subject."

Their waitress approached with two margaritas and a plate of nachos dripping with chili and cheese. Tonight was also a night void of calories or any calorie discussions. She placed the order on the table and nodded a hello to Rebecca.

Rebecca returned the older woman's warm smile. She'd known Sue Reynolds all her life, a hard worker who had put three children through college on her own. Sue was respected and loved here in Golden.

When Sue was out of earshot, Michelle sipped her drink and groaned, then said, "You never did tell me about the conversation with your mother."

"Which one?" Rebecca popped a chip into her mouth wiping the dripping cheese from her chin with a paper napkin.

"I don't know, perhaps about the abundance of sex

she had on the trip?"

"Oh right." Rebecca frowned. "I'd rather not talk about it."

Michelle almost looked hurt. "Why not?"

"I don't have the energy or the stomach and I want to enjoy my nachos."

"I guess you're right. I wouldn't want my mom talking to me about her sex life either. It's not natural."

Rebecca nodded.

"So what else is wrong?"

"Wrong?"

"You look very tired. Is something bothering you?"

Rebecca stifled a yawn. Come to think of it, she really hadn't slept well last night. Leave it to Michelle to detect when something threw her off balance.

But then why wouldn't she? Throughout their lives they had confided in each other, consoled each other, and cheered each other on so many times, it had become second nature to read each other's minds. Rebecca dipped into her purse and pulled out her compact.

"I didn't sleep well last night."

She concealed the dark shadows with a dab of makeup and blended it in. Then she snapped the compact shut. Dark circles camouflaged, she felt better.

"I figured as much. I also had a busy day what with the flu nabbing everyone in sight, I'm exhausted."

She sipped her margarita and wiped her mouth. "My desk is piled with work."

"That's a good thing, no?"

"Yes, of course it is, although I wish some of the jobs I got were larger."

"Do you need help? Because I could loan you some

money to tide you over."

"No. No. I'm fine. Call me a worrywart, but paying my bills has always been my number one priority. And when I'm not bringing in at least double my expenses, I grow concerned."

Michelle shook her head. "You work too hard."

"Look who's talking."

"I repeat, is everything okay?"

Rebecca nodded. "Aside from not sleeping well, fine. I think I've been trying to get too much done too fast. I guess, I just need to slow down."

"That's all?"

Rebecca sipped her coffee. "Sure."

"And you don't think Travis' return to town has anything to do with your inability to obtain a good night's sleep?" Michelle laughed.

Great. If Michelle jumped to conclusions, would it only be a matter of time before everyone else in town did the same? Maybe accepting Travis' job wasn't such a good idea after all.

"No. I don't. As a matter of fact I haven't thought about him until just now. Thanks so much."

Michelle flashed an I-meant-well smile.

"Fine, Travis doesn't have anything to do with your restless night. Did he *do* anything at all to you?" Michelle playfully wiggled her eyebrows.

And although Rebecca knew her friend meant no harm, she wasn't in the mood for any sort of Travis humor. Not now. It had been a long day. "He did come to my shop today, but his visit pertained to business. He asked me to redecorate his daughter's room as well as the rest of the old Victorian on Main Street he bought. You know better than anyone that I want nothing to do with him otherwise."

"Then why accept the job?" Michelle rolled her eyes. "Oh, right. I forgot about that nasty habit of yours of taking on more than you should."

"I couldn't let that beautiful Victorian slip through my hands."

"Just the Victorian?" Michelle teased.

"Very funny."

Michelle chomped on a cheesy nacho. "I ran into him the day before yesterday at the drugstore. We talked. He's changed."

"We've all changed. What's your point?"

"You know me, I'm not one to meddle."

Hah!

"I just can't help think Travis' return might be the best thing that ever happened to you."

Rebecca rolled her eyes. Michelle was way off base on this one. "Do yourself a favor. Get any ideas you have about Travis McGill and me out of your head. Our relationship is and will remain, strictly professional."

****

After school the next day, Liz slammed the back door and stomped into the kitchen. "I hate this town!" Her shrill cry tore right though Travis.

He glanced up from the new laptop he'd just downloaded software onto. An hour ago he couldn't wait for her to come home so he could see the smile on her face when he presented it to her. Now, in the mood she was in, he didn't know what her response would be.

Instead of yelling surprise and pointing to the laptop, he tapped the keyboard lightly with his index finger while deciding how to deal with the latest crisis.

He'd already learned that if he opened his mouth too fast to rebut whatever came out wouldn't be good. Not having a clue what to say and afraid of reacting too quickly, he pushed a bowl of honey roasted peanuts toward her. "Peanut?"

She stared back at him in horror. "Peanut? Look at me. I'm a whale and you want me to eat?"

He glanced at her, standing in front of him with her hands on her hips, kept his tone firm and patted the kitchen chair beside him. "Sit."

She collapsed into the chair.

"You. Are. Not. A. Whale."

"Every girl in this town is skinnier than me. They all wear these little pastel bunny jackets with white fluffy trim." She took a deep breath and dropped her backpack on the floor. It sounded like it was filled with a hundred pounds of rocks.

"What do you carry in there?"

Disbelief draped her face. "Uh, books?"

He shook his head and chose to ignore her belligerence. He'd win the bigger battles. He hoped.

"I stick out like—like, oh it's awful. And every one of them has the matching mittens, scarf, and hat. It's like they're part of a cult. And if you don't have the same thing—oh I give up."

Travis mind flew back to the chapter he'd read in a parenting self help book just the other day, teenagers and their desperate need to fit in. Yes sir, he'd started reading self-help books for parents of teenagers. Could anyone blame him? Every day with Liz was a new surprise. Half the time he said the wrong thing and the other half of the time she ignored him. After all he was *only* her father, what did he know?

She slumped further down into her seat and mumbled, "I'll never fit in here." She paused for a moment. "And they're all so—cute."

"You're cute."

"Oh, please. You have to say that because you're my dad."

He leaned his elbows on the table and studied his daughter's pouting face. He tried another angle. "What did the girls wear in Chicago?"

"Whatever they wanted. It wasn't as big a deal out there as it is here."

Travis chuckled. That was hard to believe. The beige suede boots she sported were the perfect example. As she had put it, she just *had* to have them. Everyone had them. Kids. They must have invented selective thinking and hearing.

"You find my misery amusing?"

"No. I'm just surprised to discover that Golden, Pennsylvania is the fashion capital of the world."

She stood and retrieved two sodas from the refrigerator. She opened the cans and handed one to Travis. Then she popped a peanut into her mouth.

"So what do you want to do about your fashion *faux pas*?" Travis asked once she seemed to calm down.

"You're a real card, you know that?"

"Sorry, I'll be serious now."

"I did meet a girl today. She told me she got her jacket at a shop called the Ski Hut in the mall. I'd really like one."

"Sure. Oh and before I forget, I'd like to start giving you some weekly spending money." He reached into his back pocket for his wallet.

She waved off his offer. "I don't need it. Back

home I baby sat and got paid very well." She folded her arms and stared out the kitchen window. "I was thinking I could probably start baby sitting here, too. Kids like me."

He glanced at her and smiled. "Of course they do. Why not put some flyers in the neighbor's mailboxes?"

She nodded. "Not a bad idea."

"So how about I just leave the money pinned to the bulletin board?" He nodded toward the wall by the refrigerator then put his wallet in his back pocket.

"Whatever," she mumbled. "I already have enough money for the jacket, I just need a ride."

Travis crooked his finger in her direction. She leaned in toward him.

He spoke softly. "How about you and I make a deal?"

Apprehension cloaked her face. "What kind of deal?"

"You spend the money you earn babysitting on stuff like CD's, makeup, or anything else you need. But I'm your father so I buy the essentials like food and clothing. That kind of deal."

Deflated, she looked down at her hands and sighed. *This couldn't be easy for her.* Asking him for essentials when her mom had provided them all these years had to be tough. Sure he had sent child support. But as far as Liz was concerned, Bridgett had paid for everything.

But life had changed for both of them, and she lived with him now. And the minute he had picked Liz up in Chicago, stronger parenting instincts than he ever expected to have, kicked in and he wanted to do nothing else but provide for her.

"I have homework."

He closed the laptop. "Here. Take this with you."

"Huh?"

"Consider it an early Christmas present. I figured you'd need it for school. It's also got an internal wireless card. Just let me know what email address you want so I can notify our provider."

He met her eyes. They were full of tears.

Now what had he done?

Her voice was barely audible as she played with her hands. "You can't *buy* me."

Travis leaned his elbows on the table and placed his head in his hands. They'd spent a few days together and he had opened his heart to her. How did she manage to keep her distance? Or had she just built herself a wall and chosen to hide behind it? Fear gripped him. Would she ever allow him to get close to her? Ever?

He cleared his throat. "I'd never do that."

"I think you would try."

"You're wrong." He turned and looked at her. "Look, we only have each other now."

"I only ever had Mom."

"I'm sorry I wasn't there for you. But my work kept me in New York. I'm here now, Liz. Doesn't that mean anything?"

She shook her head and walked up the stairs. A moment later, she slammed her bedroom door.

Travis remained sitting for only a moment when something inside snapped. He strode up the stairs, opened her door, and marched inside. She sat on her bed staring into space.

He placed the laptop on her bed and paced with his hands on his hips. "Liz, you may not believe me, but our new living arrangement scares the hell out of me, too. And I will not allow you to judge everything I do for you. Let me assure you, I am not trying to buy your affection."

She met his gaze.

He walked over and looked out the bay window that faced the backyard and the two acres of wooded lot that surrounded the house. Her room had a great view of the mountains and their snow covered peaks. Travis pictured the garden they would plant in spring and the trellis that would lead up to her window. He wanted it to be beautiful for her.

He nodded toward the computer. "I *want* you to have it. I know you need one for school." Besides, he and Bridgett had talked about getting her one this Christmas. "Nothing I give you will ever be intended as a bribe."

Outside her room his hands shook.

Damn. He'd blown it and probably pushed her further away. He hoped it wasn't too late for both of them to start over.

****

With the sun, the next morning brought promise.

Liz bounded down the stairs into the kitchen. "When can we go to the Ski Hut?"

Travis almost spilled his coffee. Man. He'd have to learn to bounce back faster from the whole female hormone thing—especially if he intended to live through the next few years with Liz under the same roof. He cleared his throat. "Whenever you like."

"Today? After school?" She filled a bowl with nut covered raisin cereal and milk and began to chew.

"Sure."

"After we get a Christmas tree?"

He answered wearily. "Okay."

"What?"

He didn't want to push her. "We can wait on the tree. There's plenty of time."

She studied him. "This will be my first Christmas without Mom."

Travis nodded.

"We always got a great tree. I want to. She'd want me to. Besides, the ornaments from Aunt Cecile came. I want every one of them on the tree. It'll be like she's here, you know?" She pointed to the boxes by the door that had arrived via UPS.

Travis placed his hand on her shoulder. He cleared his throat and broke the silence that hung in the room like an eight hundred pound gorilla.

"Okay, so we'll go shopping."

Now there were five words he never thought he'd hear himself say. But for his daughter he'd do anything. Even trek through the mall packed with Christmas shoppers.

Later that day inside the Ski Hut, Travis wiped beads of perspiration from his forehead. How long did it take to try on clothes? If Liz didn't emerge from the dressing room soon she'd find him passed out on the floor. How did people work here? This place was hotter than an oven.

He tugged at his turtleneck. "Liz, any time soon?"

At his request, the most beautiful green eyes he'd ever seen peeked out from behind the bright blue curtain. She laughed while she pointed at him. Seated in a chair two sizes too small for his large body, he didn't doubt he looked comical. For the second time since she had arrived in Golden, his daughter was giggling.

Seeing her eyes dance and her cheeks glow, gave Travis hope. Liz's laughter was contagious. He chuckled and stretched his long legs out before him. "Well, are you going to let me see what you tried on?"

She pulled the curtain open to reveal a light blue ski jacket with white fur trim and matching bib ski pants. "This one's my favorite."

His, too. The blue showed off her red hair and her green eyes. His daughter's beauty took his breath away.

Liz twirled in front of the full-length mirror, and spun around to face him.

Travis guessed his face gave him away.

"You like it?"

"I love it." His voice was low. "You look—" He paused and prayed he hadn't upset her again. Things had been going so well today. How long would it take him to think before he spoke?

"Like Mom?"

He nodded.

"That's a great compliment." After a moment she asked, "Did you love her?"

Travis almost fell out of the small chair. This kid thought nothing of throwing random questions one after the other. You'd think he would be prepared by now.

"In my own way." Bridget had given him the greatest gift anyone ever could—Liz, and for that he would always love her.

Yes, he and Bridgett had loved each other; they'd just never been in love with each other. But then there had only been one woman Travis had ever really fallen in love with.

"Then why did you guys get a divorce? If you and

Mom loved each other, shouldn't that have been enough?"

For anyone else it might have been. But Travis and Bridgett's relationship had been different. How could he begin to explain their relationship without making Liz feel like her birth was an accident?

Travis looked down at his hands. This wasn't the time or the place for this conversation. He wished he could change the subject, but when he lifted his face she was still studying him. Her green eyes searched for answers. "I really need to know the truth."

Travis was torn. The truth was exactly what he wanted to tell her. But if he did, he risked her not understanding. How did he explain that he had made a mistake that night he slept with Bridgett yet Liz's birth had been the most wonderful thing that had ever happened to him? Even he knew it was too much for her to grasp at her young age.

She was only fifteen. His double standard wouldn't make sense to her—perhaps when she was older. He and Liz had made some major headway over the past few days. The last thing he wanted was to damage their progress with an answer that would send her reeling. There had been times this week when they had argued and he'd been left to wonder if Liz even liked him. After this conversation, she could wind up hating him.

He drew a breath and looked up into her eyes.

"The truth."

He had never been a betting man. But today he decided to take a chance. If she was old enough to ask the question, he should at least try and answer it.

"When two people love each other it should be enough. But to be fair, they can't just love each other.

They need to be in love with each other. And your Mom and I—well, we weren't in love."

"Why?"

Ahhh. Innocence. He shrugged. "It just never happened."

His daughter studied him for a few minutes longer and smiled. "I know the two of you *had* to get married."

Travis cringed. "Did your mom tell you that?"

"I did the math, Dad."

He nodded. Okay. It could have been worse. They could have decided not to marry leaving her feeling unwanted.

From the moment Bridgett had broken the news of her pregnancy to Travis that was exactly what he hadn't wanted—his child feeling unloved, or the mother of his child feeling abandoned and alone. All those years ago his mother had never been right after his father left. *Nobody deserved to be abandoned.*

"Anyway, I guess in the long run, I'm glad you got divorced when I was little."

"Why?"

She turned and looked at herself in the mirror and shrugged. "When you're small you don't understand what's happening. You just accept your parent's decision and move on. After all, you're a little kid. You have no control over anything that happens to you."

"Good point."

"Although, I remember missing you for a long time after you left. I cried almost every night."

He caught his daughter's solemn expression in the mirror.

Ouch.

"I came and visited."

"I know. But it wasn't the same as having you there." She paused. "You and Mom have taught me something really important."

He leaned back and crossed his arms. *This kid never ceased to amaze him.* "What's that?"

"When I do get married, I'm going to make sure I'm in love with the guy right from the start."

His daughter smiled at him, planted a kiss on his cheek, and headed back into the fitting room to change back into her clothes.

At this moment, he didn't think he could love her more.

Chapter Eight

On Christmas Eve, Rebecca closed the shop early and headed into the town square for some last minute shopping with Michelle. Earlier today, there had been talk of snow but even that possibility didn't lighten her mood.

A couple walked by, staring into each other's eyes, lost in a their own world. Rebecca couldn't help gazing at them with envy.

People packed the sidewalks and Christmas carolers on the corner sang about a silent night. A small child raced in and out of the crowd followed by what appeared to be his big sister threatening to tell his mother on him if he didn't come back. Michelle grabbed her arm, "Watch out. You'll get plowed down."

Rebecca shrugged and turned her coat collar up. "You don't have that much to buy, do you? I just want to go home."

"Did Pete stop by the other night? Chris and I got an eight-foot spruce. It smells divine."

"Uh huh."

Pete Drucker owned the local greenhouse and sold Christmas trees every year. Like clockwork, he showed up at her doorstep every year. His trees were full, lush and smelled heavenly. When he'd come to her door, she didn't have the heart to say no thanks this year and ten minutes later a six-foot fir tree sat in her living room. The holiday spirit hadn't graced her this year and all she wanted to do was sleep until the new year.

Rebecca nodded. "Everyone has someone, even my mother. What's wrong with me?"

"Since when do you care who has whom? You're an independent, successful business woman. Isn't that your usual mantra?"

"Don't make fun."

"I'm sorry. I guess I take a lot for granted. I have Chris to go home to."

Rebecca's heart ached. "I don't know why I'm feeling so melancholy this year."

Michelle's shoulders slumped. "I do."

"Feel free to share."

Michelle nodded. "Travis."

Rebecca groaned. It was true. Ever since he'd come back to town she'd felt unnerved, and no matter how much she told herself nothing would ever happen between them again, she couldn't shelve this attraction that still existed, still ate at her gut, reminding her just how much he'd meant to her all those years ago.

"Come on. Let's get my shopping done. Then we'll have an early dinner and a glass of champagne."

"I'm not in the mood."

Michelle linked her arm through Rebecca's. "Well get in the mood, girlfriend, my treat. Let's go."

The two women made their way through the middle of town where the crowds were thicker than ever and on almost every corner, a Santa in his red suit rang his bell and hollered, "Merrrry Christmas!" The last jolly round fellow had caught Rebecca off guard when he rang his bell in front of her face, and yelled his greeting right in her ear. Yikes, could he be louder?

For the next three hours, bogged down with shopping bags, Rebecca followed her friend like a little dog in and out of every conceivable store, weaving through masses of people straining to be heard over music and very unhappy children.

Rebecca almost growled, “What the heck are all these kids doing out this late?”

Michelle turned to study her. “Christmas is a state of mind. Get your mind in the state, please. I hate seeing you so grumpy.”

She ignored her friend’s comment. “Seriously, with kids acting like that wouldn’t you leave them home?”

Michelle reached across the counter and handed a salesgirl a black cashmere scarf. “I’ll take this one.” With a shrug she offered, “If I had a sitter, sure.”

“Oh, I didn’t think of that.” Still there had to be a better way than dragging your unhappy child through masses of people. Couldn’t they shop on the Internet? Have everything shipped to their homes?

Perusing the long list she’d been checking off, Michelle said, “I think I’m done.”

“Thank God. My feet hurt.” The boots she wore would have been so much more comfortable if they didn’t have six-inch heels. Still, they were too pretty to pass up.

The salesgirl handed Michelle her package, and the two of them headed toward the exit. “Ready for some champagne?”

“Actually, I am.”

They stopped at Lucky Leo’s and slid into the first available booth. Michelle ordered for them as Rebecca slid out of her coat and headed toward the ladies room.

Mid-stride she froze. A couple all canoodled up, sat at a table for two in the back—and even though it was poorly lit, she recognized them immediately. Her mother and Benjamin were kissing and touching and Jesus H. Christ she had to get the hell out of here. She spun around and headed back to Michelle, who was surrounded by a few mutual friends. Which was good because Rebecca hated the thought of running out and leaving her friend alone.

Pushing her arms into her coat Rebecca wrapped her scarf around her neck. "I can't stay. I've got to go."

"What's wrong?"

"I completely forgot I have to do something..." She grabbed the one bag that was hers. "Bye everyone." She met Michelle's gaze for a brief moment. "I'll call you tomorrow."

"Wait, Becc, what did you forget?"

Rebecca didn't answer. Instead she plowed through the front door, bile rising in her throat. A cold blast of winter wind smacked her in the face but did little to refresh her. She mumbled, "I think I'm going to be sick."

When she arrived home, Sherlock greeted her with a woof, his tail wagging in anticipation of being picked up. And in the way only he could the little dog lightened her heart with one simple gesture. She sat on the sofa as he showered her chin with kisses. His little tongue tickled and Rebecca giggled.

She hugged him to her chest and breathed a deep sigh. It was true what they said about animals and their ability to lower one's blood pressure as well as raise their spirits. Whenever she was with this magnificent little dog, her mood rose. "Thank you, Sherlock." She kissed him on his cold wet nose. His little tail spun round and round as she placed him on the floor.

He followed her to the kitchen where she pulled a treat from his jar and handed it to him. He gripped the treat and tore off for his bed in the living room where he'd devour the pepperoni stick in one point three seconds flat.

She slipped off her boots and slid onto a stool in the kitchen overlooking the living room. A bottle of white wine on the counter beckoned. She filled a glass and sipped. The smell of evergreen filled Rebecca's condo, and for the first time since the tree had been delivered she breathed in the fresh clean pine and allowed it to instantly relax her. With renewed energy she filled Sherlock's dinner bowl, pushed all thoughts of her mother and Benjamin from her mind and set to work.

She walked inside, turned the radio on and adjusted the volume. Soft holiday music filled the space. She retrieved a few plastic bins filled with lights and ornaments from the guestroom closet then pulled the ladder from the hall closet and got to work. Small twinkle lights always made her feel better. She paused for a moment. She hadn't hung any twinkling lights at the shop this holiday. Could that be one of the reasons she hadn't felt in the holiday mood?

It didn't matter because she was in the Christmas mood now, so she focused on her tree. Three hours later, she stepped back and appreciated all her hard work. The Christmas tree was lovely. Sherlock nudged her leg with his paw.

She sank into her sofa and patted her lap. Sherlock was on the sofa and in her lap a moment later. For a moment, they just sat there, mesmerized by the lights and their reflection on her heirloom ornaments.

Sherlock jumped off the sofa and looked in the direction of her bedroom. Rebecca laughed. “You are such an old man. If we don’t adhere to your schedule you aren’t happy.” Sherlock went to sleep every night by eleven o’clock. Since she’d been busy with the Christmas tree he’d humored her and allowed her to linger a little later than usual. She checked the clock on the table. It was eleven forty-five.

His little tail wagged and he barked in response. She walked her wine glass over to the kitchen sink, passing her phone in its cradle on her way. Looking at Sherlock she said, “I’ll be right there. I have to do one more thing.”

Sherlock understood and scooted into her bedroom. Rebecca dialed her mother’s number and waited.

“Hellooo?”

“Mom?”

“Oh, sweetheart, I’m glad you called. We waited for you, and when you didn’t show up, I grew concerned.” The alarm in her mother’s voice made Rebecca’s heart ache.

“I know, Mom, I’m sorry.”

God that felt good to say. Not showing up for a drink with her and Benjamin more than made her worry, and Rebecca didn’t like how she’d been acting lately. Immature and childish, and that was going to change. Now.

“I want you to meet Benjamin.”

Rebecca swallowed hard. “I want to meet him, too.” And this time, she meant it. It didn’t matter what Rebecca thought of their public display of affection, it didn't matter what she thought at all, right now, all that mattered was her showing her mother she supported her. After all, she'd always there for her whenever she'd needed her.

"Can we still expect you tomorrow night?"

"Yes, of course. I look forward to it." She'd promised she would stop by for a drink and hors d'oeuvres on her way to Michelle's Christmas party.

"Oh good...sweetheart, are you all right?

Her mother's sincerity warmed her to the core. "Yes, I'm fine, just a little tired." She yawned. "I just finished decorating my tree."

"Well, that's wonderful."

She smiled because she could actually hear the happiness in her mother's voice.

"Decorating the tree was always one of your favorite things to do."

"It is, isn't it?"

"Of course, sweetheart. Well, you get a good night's sleep. I love you."

"I love you too, Mom." Placing the phone into its cradle she realized just how lucky she was to have her mom alive, healthy, happy, and enjoying every moment of her life.

****

The most special time for Travis and Liz was Christmas Eve when they decorated their tree together. As promised, Cecile had sent the boxes with the ornaments Bridgett had collected over the past few decades. Liz stressed that it wouldn't be Christmas without a part of her mom present. And to Liz, those ornaments represented a large part of her life with her mother. Travis watched as she painstakingly hung each and every one, handling it as if it were made of gold.

Once Liz had added her ornaments, Travis contributed the ones he'd purchased over the years onto the seven-foot blue spruce that now took up residence next to the family room hearth. Both of them sat gazing at the tree with its gleaming white lights. Travis had never spent that much time putting up a tree but Liz was determined to get it just right. Looking at it now, he appreciated her eye for detail and found himself regretting the thought of taking it down in a few weeks.

Liz wiped a tear from her eye. "Mom would have loved it."

Travis hugged her tightly.

A few minutes later he brought a smile to her face by surprising her with a lovely gold locket he had found in an antique store. At first he had thought the piece might be a little too mature for her. But when the clerk showed him how he could insert two photographs inside the locket, Travis didn't hesitate to buy it. He figured the worst scenario was that Liz would save it to wear when she got older.

He had gone to a photo shop and had pictures of Liz and Bridgett printed to match the size of the delicate oval openings in the locket. Like a little kid, excitement spread through him.

To his delight, she was thrilled with the gift. "I'll never take it off."

She turned around so Travis could fasten it around her neck. Relief pulsed through him. Maybe this was a sign. A sign that he was beginning to be more in tune to her likes and dislikes.

She certainly hadn't taken long to know what he liked. When she presented him with a new pair of fleece lined slippers he was touched. "Yours are ancient," she'd said.

Okay, so it didn't take a rocket scientist to see that his slippers were beyond worn. But he was a man caught up in taking care of his daughter and replacing his old slippers hadn't even crossed his mind. Liz was his only priority.

He watched her drop his old slippers into the trash and laughed at the ease with which she did so. Offering to refill his coffee mug she flitted into the kitchen. Alone with his thoughts, Travis realized how lucky he was to have her in his life. Losing Bridgett had been hard on Liz, but he'd been there for his daughter. Patience, understanding, and unconditional acceptance were traits he hoped he showed and traits he relied on to help him through each day.

****

On Christmas Day, Rebecca stopped by her mother's as promised. Her breath caught in her throat after she entered the house. Although she'd always had a way of making the holidays special, this year Mom's house seemed even warmer. Twinkling lights lit up the banister, stuffed antique Santas dressed every nook, perfectly wrapped gifts waited under the tree that looked as if it had been professionally decorated. Benjamin turned out to be a gentlemen personified, and Rebecca couldn't help be touched by the soft, gentle, loving way he treated her mother. Who the hell was she to judge their feelings? If they said they were in love, so be it. She spent a little over an hour tasting Benjamin's hors d'oeuvres.

Turns out he had been head chef in one of Chicago's top restaurants after culinary school.

Rebecca pushed her plate away and sipped her wine. "I can't eat another bite."

Leigh had slipped into the kitchen to check on yet more food. Who was she feeding, an army?

Benjamin looked disappointed. "That's too bad. The crab puffs aren't done and your mother told me they were your favorite."

He'd made her favorite appetizer? How sweet. "That was very nice of you, thank you."

"Tell you what, I'll wrap some up and you can take them home."

"That would be great."

"I'm sorry you can't stay longer. My son and his family will be here in a few hours."

"Perhaps I can meet them some other time."

Rebecca's mother reentered the room wiping her hands on a kitchen towel. "Of course you'll meet them, sweetheart. At the wedding you'll get to meet all of Benjamin's family."

Rebecca froze. She'd just digested the fact that they'd be living together. Call her old-fashioned, but was her mother trying to kill her?

Leigh slipped onto the sofa beside her. "We were thinking a July wedding would be beautiful. What do you think?"

Think? I can barely breathe. "Whatever you want, Mom. Whatever both of you want." Rebecca quickly slipped her arms into the sleeves of her coat. "I should run." I should sprint, I should fly. I should get the hell out of here.

Benjamin handed her a bag. "I wrapped the crab puffs for you."

She couldn't dislike this man, no matter how much

she wanted. He was kind, sweet, and damn it, sincere.

"Thank you, Benjamin. It's been wonderful meeting you." She reached out to shake his hand and he gently pulled her into a hug. His spicy, woodsy aftershave gripped her senses and Rebecca's eyes misted. She slowly pulled away but not before he noticed her sad expression.

"Are you all right, Rebecca?"

"Do you...do you wear Old Spice?"

His smile was warm and large. "I do."

So did my father. For years. She nodded. "Very nice."

She hugged her mother, said goodnight and headed to her car as realization hit her. Her mother had fallen in love with a man just like her father. She placed the key into the ignition and smiled. "Well done, Mom."

****

New Year's Eve had been quiet and uneventful. Travis and Liz spent the evening at home watching the Times Square special on the tube. Over the break, he'd learned to put everything aside whenever Liz made an appearance. So full of life, he didn't want to miss a moment of their time together. In all honesty, Travis was glad Liz would be returning to school today. Living with a fifteen-year-old female got old fast.

He sat at his favorite stool at the kitchen counter drinking coffee and reading the paper when Liz bounded into the room drawing all his attention.

Today, he was the one who had the first news of the day. "Don't forget, you're meeting with Rebecca after school at her shop."

Liz's eyes glowed. "Yes!"

Travis didn't care how long the process took. Liz

was coming out of her shell and deep down he figured it had a lot to do with her visits with Becca. They were becoming friends and he knew how important a positive female role model was in his daughter's life. He wondered if Becca realized how fond Liz had grown of her and what high regard she held her.

After a few bites of her cereal she grabbed her backpack. "See you later." She glanced at his feet before heading out the back door. "Nice slippers."

"Yes, they are," he hollered. As Travis watched her leave, a feeling of complete contentment filled him. He and Liz had been doing okay on their own and for a guy with very little parenting experience, he had to admit, he wasn't handling things too badly.

****

Later that afternoon, Rebecca was glad to be back at work with the holidays over. Mike had always made New Year's Eve special combining Annie's birthday party with bringing in the new year. With both of them gone, she no longer celebrated. Instead, she climbed into bed pulled the covers up and cried herself to sleep.

In the backroom where she stored all the fabric books, frustration niggled. Rebecca found it almost impossible to locate a coordinating fabric for Mrs. Wofford's Queen Anne dining room chairs. One would think a task as simple as reupholstering six dining room chairs could be done in no time. But Mrs. Wofford wanted what Mrs. Wofford wanted, and so far, the only choices available were solids and tone-on-tone fabrics. Rebecca sighed. Talking her stubborn client into an elegant solid would prove impossible.

Researching another option for the older woman would take hours, so when Elizabeth McGill with her red curly shoulder length hair and bright green eyes, bounced into the shop, Rebecca's project for Mrs. Wofford immediately took a back seat.

Looking at the smile plastered on the teen's face Rebecca was taken aback by how much of a striking resemblance she held to her father. She wondered if Travis realized.

After their usual hellos, Rebecca led Liz to a table containing dozens of fabric books, paint chip samples, and wallpaper books that she had laid out ahead of time for this visit.

"Okay. Today it's down to business."

Rebecca had let Elizabeth call the shots during their past appointments. She'd been relaxed and casual, but they always ended up talking about Elizabeth's life and never about her bedroom project. Instead they'd leafed through books and discussed colors, never making a definite choice of any kind. She had hoped the young girl would find something she liked, that grabbed her attention, so they could get her project started.

Since that hadn't been the case, Rebecca decided to take matters into her own hands. Not only was she looking forward to finishing Elizabeth's room and seeing her face light up with happiness, she couldn't wait to get started renovating the rest of their house.

First things first she reminded herself. She tucked the fact that they needed to complete Elizabeth's room before they could move on into the back of her mind and dealt with the issue at hand.

Elizabeth nodded. "Right. Business."

Good. Cooperative was always good. The teen's smile penetrated right through Rebecca.

"No more guessing. No more changing your mind. Your father is probably wondering why we haven't done anything to that room of yours yet."

Elizabeth fiddled with her fingers. "Not really."

"Sure he is."

"I think he just likes that I'm here with you." Elizabeth's eyes met Rebecca's. "I know I like it."

Rebecca swallowed hard as warmth spread through her. "Me too, sweetie, but admit it. Wouldn't you love your room to be finished the way you like it?"

Elizabeth remained quiet.

Rebecca reached across the table and touched the young girl's hand. "You can stop in anytime to see me. Finishing your bedroom or the renovation of your house doesn't mean we can't spend time together."

Elizabeth's eyes radiated happiness. "Right. So let's get started."

Relief flooded Rebecca. Honestly, she couldn't imagine Elizabeth not stopping in every day after school. The teenager had filled a void in her life and for that Rebecca was grateful.

"What's your absolute favorite color? The color you just can't live without?"

When Elizabeth blurted, "Blue," Rebecca wasn't the least bit surprised. Half of the young girl's wardrobe was blue. "Light, medium, or dark?"

"Medium."

Rebecca spread five fans of medium blue paint on the table before Elizabeth. She had guessed right. "Look through these and let me know what you think."

Worry creased Elizabeth's forehead. "Wow. There are so many."

"Don't get overwhelmed. You'll know which one's

your favorite by eliminating one at a time." Rebecca smiled and left Elizabeth alone to thumb through the samples.

Ten minutes later, bubbling with excitement, Elizabeth called, "I found it! The perfect blue."

"It's beautiful. Now let's talk about the windows and bedding."

"I don't want anything too fruffy."

"Nothing fruffy. Got it." Rebecca sketched a balloon valance with drapery panels.

Elizabeth leaned in to watch.

"Now. I'm thinking this style will work beautifully on the bay window opposite your bed that overlooks the mountains. Of course the fabric you choose will decide just how feminine the treatment becomes."

Elizabeth frowned. "Huh?"

"A floral will make the treatment more feminine than a check or a paisley."

Elizabeth shook her head. "No paisley. Jen, my friend back home? Her mom used it in her husband's office and it looks way manly."

Rebecca nodded. "As it should. Paisleys tend to be masculine. For your room, however, I was thinking we could use two or three coordinating fabrics. For example, a floral, a check and a small dot."

"I like that."

Over the next hour they thumbed through a multitude of fabric books. Rebecca was relieved when no one came in or out of the shop during their time together. The girl was on a roll and Rebecca didn't want an interruption to throw off her concentration.

Upon completion, they'd chosen three colors: medium blue, celery green and pale violet. A vivid medium scale floral combined all three colors for Elizabeth's comforter; a check with the same three colors would work for the cornice board and window seat cushion, and a small violet dot for the drapery panels and bed skirt. Pillows in celery green, medium blue and violet would accent the bed. About an hour later they hugged and said goodbye. Rebecca had never felt better about any job she'd worked on.

Chapter Nine

The next day Rebecca called Travis. "I'd like to drop over today if that's possible. I need to measure Elizabeth's windows for the new draperies."

Since it was an older home, the windows in Travis' house had been installed during the early 1900's. And even though he planned to replace them all, each was wider and taller than the more up-to-date models built during the last decade.

Travis' hesitation made Rebecca bite her bottom lip. *Great, another awkward moment.*

At first she thought she could wait until Elizabeth returned from school for the day, walk over with her, let the girl help her measure the windows. But after reviewing her schedule, there just wasn't time. This morning was her only available slot.

"Sure," he said finally. "I have to run to the office and pick up a few things in about an hour. Can you come over before then?"

"I'm on my way."

As she disconnected the call, she wondered why her hand was shaking. Granted, she'd not planned on seeing him today, but without her own personal key to his home, she had no choice. Besides, she'd be in and out in no time. She'd make sure of it.

****

After a quick hello to Travis, Rebecca headed

straight upstairs. It wasn't hard to locate Liz's room. The blaring bright pink paint he'd chosen almost lit up the hallway. This particular shade of pink even nauseated Rebecca, someone who loved color. What in the world had he been thinking? Thank God the painters would be here next week.

She placed the small step stool she had brought with her in front of the large window and dug inside her tote bag for a pad, pen and measuring tape. As she climbed up onto the stool to measure for the valance that would eventually mount from the ceiling, the bright early morning sun blinded her. Rebecca lost her balance and fell backwards.

Into Travis' arms.

His hands held her too tightly and his grin unnerved her. Her mind flashed back to the spring of their senior year in high school. Apple picking at one of the local orchards, Travis had caught her in a similar way when she had lost her footing. Back then it had all been playful and they had embraced and kissed with longing, need, desire. It had been nice, then.

Now Rebecca wiggled crazily in an attempt to free herself. She didn't need memories of their past clouding her mind and her judgment. She didn't need his holding her so close his aftershave tantalized her, and she didn't need him sneaking up on her pretending to play hero.

She didn't need him at all, damn it.

He placed her gently on the floor. "Where did you come from?" she huffed and pulled her shirt into place.

"Don't you mean, thanks for catching me?"

She brushed herself off. She shouldn't be mad at him. He had done her a favor. She had been too wrapped up in her task and might have sustained an injury that set her back weeks. Still, she didn't like being taken by surprise. And the warm feelings coursing through her more than upset her. "Look, I don't need any help."

"Yeah, I could see that."

She tried to gather her dignity, but it was hard when her shirt had ridden all the way up her middle. Rebecca ran her hands through her hair in a lame attempt to calm herself.

"I came up here to give you a key."

She must have looked confused because he added, "To the house."

When she took the key from him, their fingers touched and gazes locked. After a long uncomfortable moment, she said, "Thanks for catching me."

"My pleasure. I thought having your own key might come in handy."

She nodded, staring at the key in her sweaty palm.

"For dropping in *whenever* you need to."

His emphasis on the word whenever, unnerved her.

"Travis, I assure you, the only reason I would use this key is for professional reasons."

"Of course, why else?"

"Right."

Luckily she was facing the window and he couldn't see the red blaze of her cheeks. She nodded. "I should finish here."

She didn't exhale until she heard the front door click closed behind him.

****

As Travis started his truck, the sweet aroma of Becca's hair continued to tease his senses. He pushed any urges of a personal nature aside and thought practically. Thank God he had walked in when he did or she might have hurt herself. He put the vehicle into drive and pulled out onto the street.

On the drive to his office, his thoughts revolved around Becca. With her being stubborn to the core, her thanks took him by surprise. In the old days, she would never have acknowledged that his help had come in handy—back then she played hard to get.

But he knew better. When he had her in his arms she became liquid heat. He knew how and where to touch her to send chills racing through her. And he knew talk had never been necessary to convey just how much she had meant to him.

That was then and this was now. Time had changed everything between them. It had not only felt good to hold her in his arms, it had felt right. He also knew it had been against her will. How he wished it hadn't. How he wished she had melted into his arms extinguishing the past completely. How he wished she'd thrown her arms around his neck and kissed him in the way only she could. His groin tightened with frustration.

But that wouldn't happen. Travis could still feel the tension between them and he wanted nothing more than to break down the barrier keeping them apart. Positive he had seen longing in her eyes when he had caught her, he wouldn't give up. When the opportunity presented itself, he'd kiss her, she'd melt into his arms like long ago, and finally they'd be together again.

****

On Monday, after Elizabeth met Rebecca at the shop, she handed her a few design books. "I'd like you to begin looking through these to help you get an idea of what furniture style you might like."

"Don't have to. I already know. "The teenager pulled a piece of paper from her jacket pocket, painstakingly unfolded a page torn from a magazine.

Rebecca smiled at her excitement.

"This furniture is to die for." She showed her a picture containing a light oak queen size sleigh bed with matching dresser, mirror, and armoire.

"Impressive."

Good taste for a fifteen year old. Pricy too. Since Travis would be dropping quite a bit of money to renovate the old Victorian, she'd look locally for furniture but in a similar and more affordable price range.

"You'll never believe what's in my room now...white furniture for a three-year-old." Elizabeth frowned. "It's hideous. Stuffed animals everywhere, a toy chest. Can you believe it? I don't own any toys. I mean—I'm fifteen."

Rebecca remembered the desperation on Travis' face the day he had explained his daughter's unhappiness about his choices, and hoped she might have a remedy for the problem. "There is a furniture store a few blocks away that has a bedroom set close to the one in this picture."

Elizabeth's eyes went to the size of saucers. A grin split her face. "Really?"

"Understand, it's not the same color wood. The one at the store is a deeper oak."

"That's okay. It's not the color of the wood I like as much as the style." Elizabeth's eyes practically sparkled. "Can we go and take a look at it?"

Rebecca checked the calendar on her desk. "I have

an appointment at four o'clock."

She looked up and met Elizabeth's puppy dog eyes. If they hurried, she could be back with minutes to spare. Besides, Elizabeth was on a roll, and Rebecca didn't dare stop her creative juices that presently flowed like a waterfall.

"Oh, all right. Let's go."

Travis clearly didn't deny Elizabeth anything, yet, she wasn't the least bit spoiled. There was a genuine sweetness about her that emanated from deep within. Elizabeth squealed and grabbed her backpack.

"But we must hurry."

The teenager nodded enthusiastically.

Outside the shop Rebecca told Elizabeth to call Travis and let him know where the two of them were headed. Watching the young girl excitedly tell her father that they were going furniture shopping lit Rebecca up inside.

She didn't think she could remember the last time she'd seen anyone so happy over something as silly as furniture. Wait a minute, yes she could. When she had told Travis she'd help redecorate Elizabeth's room. The same sparkle in his eyes had resembled his daughter's only a moment ago.

At the furniture store Elizabeth loved the bedroom set so they wasted no time in placing an order. She wouldn't give Elizabeth time to change her mind. No matter how much she enjoyed spending time with the teen, Rebecca was bursting to begin work on another room.

Outside the store, her cell phone rang. "No, Mrs. Galway, of course I understand. It seems as though everyone's ill with the flu right now. It's more important that you get well. Why don't you call me when you're up to it and we'll reschedule then." She dropped her cell into her coat pocket.

"Does that mean what I think?" Elizabeth asked eagerly.

"It means I no longer have a four o'clock if that's what you're hinting at."

Rebecca squinted from the sun. She swore the young girl's enthusiasm was stronger than the blinding rays glaring down on them right now. Amazing how the sun could still be so strong in the middle of winter.

"Can we shop for carpeting now?"

The teenager's eyes, so clear and bright, reflected the endless possibilities life held. Rebecca bit her bottom lip. "I think your Dad mentioned refinishing the wood floors to eliminate carpeting altogether."

"He does but I talked him into letting me carpet my room. I hate cold floors in the morning."

Rebecca didn't doubt Elizabeth had talked Travis into only carpeting her room. The girl had her father wrapped around her finger. Who was she to talk? Elizabeth had stolen her heart in the short time they had known each other. She was no different than Travis.

"Call your father first and tell him why you'll be later than planned." Rebecca led her toward the Rug Mart as Elizabeth made another quick call to Travis.

When Elizabeth hung up Rebecca asked. "Do you have a lot of homework today?"

Elizabeth shrugged and slipped one arm through Rebecca's. "I finished all of it in study hall. I have an algebra quiz tomorrow, but I can study after dinner."

Rebecca's breath caught in her throat. Elizabeth's touch reminded her just how vulnerable she was—and just how much she missed her own family. She and Mike had just started their family when he and the baby were taken so abruptly.

She squeezed Elizabeth's hand and quickened their pace. Rebecca couldn't help but have a deep admiration for her. Only fifteen year's old and Elizabeth had already made so many adjustments—-the loss of her mother, a major geographical move, a new school with new friends, living with a father she was just getting to know. Yet somehow amidst every bit of instability, Elizabeth managed to keep it all together.

After her own loss, Rebecca had taken years to rid herself of sadness. And here, Elizabeth seemed to be bouncing back to normal with such ease, Rebecca couldn't help being envious. And even though Rebecca was thrilled for the teenager who deserved happiness, she couldn't help thinking that Elizabeth was mourning more than she would admit.

Elizabeth was vibrant, full of life, and eager to seize all life put in front of her while Rebecca remained hesitant, cautious, and careful. She leaned toward her, breaking Rebecca from her daze. "How long have you lived in Golden?"

"All my life." They crossed the street and Rebecca waved to Mrs. Simpson walking her little white poodle, who proudly sported a purple faux fur coat. "Hello, Chloe," she said and made a mental note to stop at the pet store later. Sherlock was almost out of treats.

"You like dogs?" Elizabeth asked.

Rebecca smiled. "Love them. I have one of my own." She pulled out her cell phone. "This is Sherlock."

Elizabeth took the cell phone and studied the picture Rebecca had stored as her exterior wallpaper.

"He's adorable. Who watches him while you're at work?"

Rebecca thought a moment. "Well, no one. He's a good dog and he's house trained. Sometimes I run home at noon and take him out. On the days I can't, I make sure and give him extra attention when I do get home."

"I always wanted a dog."

"Allergies?"

Elizabeth shook her head. "Not me. Mom. Cats, dogs, any animal dander irritated her."

"I've been thinking of finding someone to walk Sherlock in the afternoon, get him some exercise. You interested?"

Elizabeth's eyes widened. "Are you serious?"

"Of course I am. But you'll need to ask your father first."

"No problem. So when can I start?"

"Check with him and we'll discuss it tomorrow."

"Okay."

They continued down the block. "So you've known my father a long time?"

"Long enough."

"For like—forever?"

"Well, not forever."

"But you went to high school together?"

"Yes."

"Wow."

"It's not a big deal."

A blast of cold air caused Elizabeth's light blue hood with fluffy white trim to flip off her head. She quickly tossed it back on. "I mean, he's my father and I don't really know him. Meeting someone who's known him as long as you, is—unbelievable."

"Not really. That blue is a pretty color on you."

"Thanks. Dad liked it too. So 'fess up. What was he like?"

Rebecca laughed. *This kid had a one-track mind.* "When?"

"In high school."

"Why don't you ask him?"

"Oh, yeah, as if he's going to tell me."

"He will, if you ask."

"So you knew him pretty well?"

"I used to."

"And now?"

"I haven't seen him in a very long time. So how is school?"

The teenager shrugged. "School is school." Elizabeth was quiet for a moment. "Who did my Dad date in high school?"

Rebecca's pulse quickened. "Oh, various girls."

This was one topic she was not discussing. If Travis wanted his daughter to know about his past, he would have to tell her himself. Rebecca looked up and saw they were outside the Rug Mart.

Thank God.

She pulled Elizabeth inside and a watched the teenager become engrossed in carpet choices, their conversation of a moment ago old news.

Elizabeth chose a sand colored plush carpet with thick pile for her bedroom. Rebecca couldn't contain her laughter when the young girl made it sound urgent that she had to have a rug with thick pile to sink her toes into each morning.

After the store manager promised to send someone

out on Saturday morning to measure, they left the store arm in arm, sharing a wonderful feeling of accomplishment.

Outside they ran right into Travis. His navy blue pea coat was open and blowing with the cold wind. His jeans clung to his lean hips and his gray turtleneck and red sweater made him look more appealing than Rebecca cared to admit.

"Anyone up for pizza?" he asked.

"Always," Elizabeth chimed.

"You two have fun," Rebecca said.

Elizabeth whined. "You're not coming with us?"

"Would you like us both to whine?" Travis asked.

His daughter smacked him playfully on the arm. "I am not whining."

"Oh no. You never do that."

Elizabeth shot him a beautiful smile. Rebecca watched his face light up as he pulled his daughter into his arms for a hug. Unexpected admiration for this man warmed her. He was so good with her. They were good for each other.

"Dad, we're in public."

Travis released her but not before planting a quick kiss on her forehead. He turned his attention to Rebecca. "How about joining us?"

"I would if I could. Really. But I need to get back to the shop."

"Please?"

Rebecca threw her arms into the air in surrender. What harm could there be in grabbing a soda with the two of them? Besides, she couldn't refuse the plea in Elizabeth's large green eyes. "I give up."

Travis grinned. "I love an agreeable woman."

"It can only be for a quick soda and then I have to run." To where and why, Rebecca had no idea. She just knew she wasn't ready to spend any one-on-one time with Travis. Thank goodness Elizabeth was with them.

"Hey, Dad, Rebecca asked me if I can walk her dog after school. I can, can't I?"

Travis' smile came all the way from his toes. "If you want to."

Elizabeth grinned. "If I want to? You're kidding right?" A moment later she waved to a friend across the street and within seconds she was a block ahead of them.

So much for Rebecca's built-in chaperone.

Travis shook his head. "She's something, isn't she?"

"Yes, she is."

"What kind of dog do you have?"

Rebecca spent the next few minutes describing Sherlock to Travis.

"That's not a dog. That's a mop."

Rebecca stopped walking. "You will not make fun of my dog."

Travis stepped back and tried to hide his amusement. He raised his hands showing he gave up. "I promise."

After they walked a little further he slipped his arm around Rebecca's waist and pulled her into a doorway.

She reached around and removed his hand. "What are you doing?"

"Becoming reacquainted?"

She swallowed hard. There was that lopsided grin again. Pulling her head back in surprise she asked, "Excuse me?"

"Come on, Becca, don't deny it. The attraction between us is even stronger than before." He ran the back of his hand over her cheek. "You feel it, too, don't you?"

Her skin heated under his touch. *She'd have to be dead not to feel it.*

"You're hallucinating. Do you feel all right?" She put her hand on his forehead then quickly removed it. Touching him was bad. Very bad. Her stomach quivered.

His eyes bore into hers as he leaned his hands on the brick building behind them, pinning her against it.

"Let's keep things in perspective, Travis. You are my employer, remember?"

"But you make it so difficult." His voice was low and his lips were inches from hers.

"How?"

"You make it difficult for me not to want to kiss you."

"I haven't done any such thing."

He whispered, "Oh, yes, you have." And before she knew what was happening his lips covered hers.

Rebecca wanted to push him away, but instead she felt herself lean in toward him opening her mouth as he deepened the kiss. He tasted like coffee and cookies. And she wanted to taste more, to get lost in the heat coursing through her.

She ran her hands through his hair and pulled him closer, ignoring the internal voice prompting her to stop. A groan escaped his throat. Gently he slipped his hand around her waist and pulled her against him, his need throbbing against her torso.

A moment later, breathless, she stopped. "I'm

sorry. I can't do this."

Clearly frustrated, he ran his hair through his already mussed hair. "Why?"

There were so many reasons but right now she couldn't remember one. Her voice was low, "It's not right."

"Trust me, babe. It's more than right."

"I'm working for you." She twisted her head from side-to-side to see if anyone had seen them and looked Travis in the eye.

"It's after hours."

"You said it yourself, Golden is a small town."

He winced as she threw his own words into his face. Then he sighed and shoved his hands into his pockets.

"Tell Elizabeth I'm sorry. We'll do pizza another time."

Rebecca turned and hurried down the block. *Who was she kidding, thinking Travis no longer had the power to melt her with his kisses?* She wrapped her arms around herself, and vowed she wouldn't allow him that close to her way again.

Making a sharp turn at the corner she ran right into her mother. "Sweetheart. What a nice surprise." Leigh held onto her shoulders. "What's wrong?"

"Nothing. I'm fine."

"Don't give me that." Her mother slipped her arm through hers. "Have you eaten dinner?"

"I was going to get pizza, but I changed my mind."

"Let's grab a bite, shall we?"

"Where's Benjamin?" Since they'd gotten together the two of them had become inseparable.

"He's having drinks with a friend that's in town

tonight. Isn't that perfect? Now you and I can spend some alone time together." She nodded toward Kate's Cafe. "How about we eat here?"

"Okay." Rebecca didn't have the energy to argue and she was hungry, so why not stop in and eat. When they entered the crowded bar/restaurant the warmth comforted her. Rebecca unbuttoned her coat as they waited to be seated.

Leigh's eyes darted around the establishment. "I have to bring Benjamin here. He'd love the ambiance."

Feeling her mother studying her, Rebecca avoided her gaze. The hostess seated them a moment later in a booth along the wall. After slipping out of their coats, the women ordered glasses of Chardonnay.

"So. Tell me. What's wrong?"

"I appreciate your concern, Mom, but I'd rather not talk right now."

"Ohhhh." Leigh's eyes grew big and wide. "This is about a man."

Rebecca groaned and placed her head in her hands.

"Yes and no."

"Does this have anything to do with Travis McGill?"

Rebecca's head popped up. "Why do you ask that?"

Her mother smiled at the waitress who delivered their wine. "Ready to order?"

"No. Please give us a few minutes," Leigh said.

"No problem."

When the waitress was out of earshot, Rebecca continued. "Mom?"

Leigh sipped her Chardonnay and shrugged. "No reason in particular. I saw him in the supermarket."

“Tell me you didn’t talk to him.”

Lord knows what she would have felt free to say, and Rebecca did not want Travis thinking she’d talked to her mother or anyone about him.

“Don’t worry. He didn’t see me. I know how you hate it when I interfere.”

Rebecca’s chest ached. Her mother only had good intentions. “Thank you for not saying anything to him.”

“Even if I could have. What would I say? You know, sweetheart, a lot of time has gone by since you’ve seen each other. You two should talk. Get it all out in the open and leave the past in the past.”

“I’ve already seen him, Mom.” And smelled him, and touched him, and damn I’ve even wanted him. God, I hate myself.

“That’s fabulous.”

“No. It’s isn’t.” Rebecca tasted her wine. It left a warm sensation in her throat.

Her mother leaned back in the booth and pulled her menu open. “All right. If you say so.”

Rebecca sighed. Good. Conversation over.

The waitress took their orders a few minutes later and left.

“Did I tell you Benjamin and I ordered a king sized bed last week and it was delivered yesterday?”

“No. I’m sure it’s very nice.”

“Oh, it’s beyond nice. Its so comfortable we sleep like the dead.”

Rebecca didn’t comment.

“I know you don’t like him...”

Where did she get that idea? She wasn’t in love with him, but she liked him enough and she thought given some time she would like him even more. “That’s not true. I do like him."

"Really? Why didn't you tell me?"

Rebecca shrugged. "We got along great when I came over; I thought you could see I approved."

"Oh, sweetheart, that means the world to me." Her voice was filled with relief.

Rebecca kept her own voice low. "I wish the two of you wouldn't rush into marriage, though."

Leigh frowned. "We are doing no such thing."

"You've only known each other a few weeks."

"It only takes a minute to fall in love with someone."

"I don't believe that," Rebecca whispered.

Her mother studied her freshly manicured fingernails. "So that's the story you're sticking with?"

Manicures, just another detail she'd added to her feminine mystique since the arrival of Benjamin. "What are you referring to?"

"I'm not sure you're strong enough to discuss it." Leigh's gaze darted around the restaurant.

Irritation roiled at the delaying tactic. "No, tell me. What are you talking about?"

Her mother rubbed her chin in thought. "Let's see, you were about seventeen and came home from high school so smitten and in love there was no talking to you. I believe his name was Trav..."

"Don't, Mom."

"He put you in this bad mood, didn't he?"

Rebecca shrugged. "It's my own fault."

"We can't help whom we love, sweetheart. Our hearts control that."

"I don't love him."

"Are you sure?"

"Of course I'm sure. Don't you think I'd know if I loved him?"

Heat radiated to her core. Love him? There are times I want to punch him. I can't stand close to him because I want to smack him and scream, why the hell did you screw everything up all those years ago?

"I'm just saying you loved him from the first moment you met him, and you continued to love him for many years afterward. Feelings that deep don't just disappear."

"Great advice from someone who jumps in head first." Not me. I take my time. Ever since I was burned I've become selective. Yeah, that's the word. Selective. No jumping at the first Joe who smiles my way.

"Are you trying to start an argument?"

Rebecca shook her head. "No. I'm sorry. But it seems to me that you and Benjamin are rushing into things too fast."

"At least we're putting ourselves out there and aren't scared of falling in love. Life is short, sweetheart. You of all people should know that."

"I'm not afraid of love. I loved Mike and Annie."

"Mike's gone, honey. Don't you think it's long past time you moved on with your life? He would have wanted you to. You're still young enough to remarry and have another family. Don't deny yourself a happily ever after. Travis' returning to Golden is perfect timing if you ask me."

"I'm not asking you, Mom."

"All I'm saying is you shouldn't push him away if he shows signs of wanting to get close again."

"I'm not."

"I think he's always loved you and has never

stopped."

Rebecca rolled her eyes.

She reached over and touched Rebecca's hand. "Do yourself a favor, give the man a chance."

Rebecca could only nod. It was taking all her control to hold back the tears that threatened.

"If you don't see what these feelings are all about, you will never know what could have been." Leigh then excused herself and headed toward the ladies' room.

Rebecca finished her wine as the waitress brought over their dinner. She couldn't push her mother's words from her mind, "you'll never know what could have been."

She blew out a deep sigh and squeezed ketchup onto her bacon cheeseburger. She'd never admit it, but maybe her mother was onto something. Even at her age, she was willing to get back out there.

Losing Mike and Annie had devastated her. Had she not realized and put up a shield to stop anyone else from getting close? Had she done this consciously telling herself she was fine on her own? She honestly wasn't sure.

With her mother on her way back to the table, Rebecca conceded that with age came wisdom and knowledge, and Leigh Evans never hesitated to share hers. Perhaps Rebecca would be more open over the next few weeks, and discover whether there was any truth to her statement.

Chapter Ten

The next two days passed quickly. With such a busy schedule she didn't have time for sleep much less think about Travis or what her mother said the other evening at dinner. Rebecca had more important issues to worry about—because for the first time since she had opened the doors of her decorating business she was worried. Really worried.

The only large job she had acquired in months, the renovation of the town's oldest hotel threatened to fall apart right before her eyes if she didn't do something fast. She met Michelle for lunch in search of answers.

"How long does this particular strain of flu last?" Rebecca tossed her jacket into the booth.

"It depends on the individual and how hard it hits them. Basically, it could last anywhere from six to twelve days. And this strain—the one that's hit town—this is one of the worst we've experienced in the last few years. I've never seen so many people stricken so fast." Michelle rubbed her hands together. "It's getting colder much faster this year, don't you think?"

Rebecca ran her hands through her hair in frustration. "Maybe. I really hadn't noticed. Working on Travis' renovation at the same time as the Union Hotel is driving me crazy."

Michelle shot her a look. "You were complaining about the cold the other day. What's wrong?"

"I know I agreed to help Travis, and I really want to. It's just that for the first time in my career, I might not meet an important deadline."

"You always exaggerate."

Rebecca's eyes widened. "I'm serious. All of my contractors are ill. There is no one healthy enough to paint the hotel's interior. Who would have thought something as trivial as the common cold could put me out of business?"

"It's not the common cold, it's the flu. And things like this happen."

"If I were working with anyone else on the hotel project, I would probably just go over and explain. A normal person would understand. But Mr. Morley. He is not normal." A stickler for detail, missing deadlines was unacceptable to the man.

"You'll come through."

"Maybe not this time. This is huge. It's not like I can even go over there with a bucket of paint and a roller myself. There are over two dozen rooms that need painting. With all my workers sick, my hands are tied."

"You'll find a way," Michelle reassured her. "You always do."

"Nope. The grand reopening is in another week. Nothing short of a miracle will suffice."

****

Travis sat two booths away with his back facing Becca and Michelle. Ever so slowly he slid down in his seat to avoid being spotted. He suspected if she got the slightest glimpse of him, she would immediately stop talking.

Eavesdropping wasn't his style but right now he was more than glad to be within earshot of their conversation.

Rebecca continued. “The hotel celebrates its one hundredth birthday this year. The whole town will be there.”

“Every one of your guys is ill?”

“When five of them called in, I assumed the other four would pick up the slack. Even if they had to work double time, I’d pay them. But when each of them called in, everything fell apart.”

“Even I can’t guarantee they’ll be well in a week. The flu can hit pretty hard. Explain to Mr. Morley. Some things in life are even out of his control. Even he has to have a soft spot somewhere beneath all that gruffness for life’s unexpected moments.”

She shook her head. “His assistant said he’s in Philadelphia for the day. I'll have to wait for tomorrow morning to see him—another day wasted.”

Michelle reached across the table and patted her hand. “It’ll be okay, Becc, you’ll see.”

“Morley has been preparing for this celebration for months. When I don’t complete this job he’ll spread the word through this county and the surrounding five that Designs of Distinction isn’t worth a lick. Closing the doors is just a matter of time.”

Travis bit his lip. Why hadn’t she come to him for help? He didn’t bite, did he? No. It had nothing to do with him—Becca was stubborn, stubborn and foolish.

He shook his head in disbelief. When it came to something as important as her business, she shouldn’t have thought twice about reaching out for assistance. But Travis knew her hesitation to ask for help ran deeper. She was determined to keep him at a safe distance no matter what.

Unfortunately she was right when it came to old man Morley.

Even Travis, who had only been back in town a few weeks, knew what a large influence Howard Morley had on the people of Golden. He'd served as mayor for two terms and even contemplated running for governor until his health got in the way and his wife forced him to take the job running the inn so he'd rest more. The man knew everyone. He was respected and reputed and his word was like gold.

Sure, the flu had hit a handful of his workers. But he had dozens of others who hadn't been affected and were willing to work on call. And because of that, he could have had a crew available for her in no time.

Rebecca continued, "While I'm at it, why don't I just call my brother and tell him I've decided to relocate to Jersey? I can start over there. Hell, I hardly see him and his family anyway. That's definitely something to consider."

"You're being a little extreme, don't you think?"

"Not after Morley gets done with me."

New Jersey? Absolutely not.

As long as Travis could do something to help her, she wasn't moving anywhere. He sat up, finished his coffee, and folded his newspaper. If he was going to help Becca, he needed to hurry. After all, she said Morley was only out of town today. He grabbed his jacket and turned.

Becca's face flushed a light pink. Travis pretended he had not heard a word of their conversation. "Ladies." He nodded.

"Travis," Michelle acknowledged.

"Just reading the paper. Anyone see the Eagles

game this weekend? Twenty-four to nine," he said before heading toward the door. "What a game."

When he was about a foot away he heard Michelle mutter, "Men and sports."

Travis smiled. They were clueless.

****

The next morning Rebecca woke before the sun rose over the snow-peaked mountains. Peaceful and serene the image usually soothed her. Not today.

Anger rippled through her at the unfairness of it all. Never one to fail job responsibilities, she began making phone calls to independent painters within fifty miles of Golden, offering to pay double their normal fee. And although they all seemed nice enough, no one had been free to drive to town and help her out of her predicament.

She walked out the door and headed toward Main Street, dread nipping at her heels. "Dead man walking," she muttered. Michelle met her on the way, smile on her gorgeous face. Becca stared at the cups of hot coffee in her friend's hands. "What's this?"

"Did you seriously think I'd let you face mean old Morley alone?"

Rebecca's heart filled with gratitude. Michelle was one of a kind. "Thanks."

When they entered the hotel's massive lobby they were greeted by the smell of fresh paint.

Lots and lots of fresh paint.

Rebecca's breath caught in her throat.

Mr. Morley rushed over to greet her. "Those magnificent men worked all through the night."

Rebecca's wide eyes scanned the foyer from top to bottom. The walls were coated with a creamy ivory.

Not one, but two. And the trim was done in the same semi-gloss. *Exactly according to her plans.*

She peered into the main dining room. Its walls were finished as well, only in dove gray. Just as she had written on the room chart she left for the workers by the paint cans in the hall last week. The workers who all called in sick.

Speaking of paint cans—Rebecca peeked around the corner where she left the cartons containing all the paint necessary to complete this monstrous job. They were gone.

It's a Christmas miracle.

Rebecca swallowed hard. "Pinch me, Michelle," she whispered. She walked into the room off the parlor, which had been painted the palest of blues.

Mr. Morley continued, "When I heard so many people in town were sick with the flu, I have to admit, I began to worry. What with our grand reopening merely one week away—I began to think there was no way you'd meet the deadline and we wouldn't be able to celebrate the hotel's anniversary. Well, not in the original intended style."

Rebecca couldn't figure out what had happened. What men had worked through the night into this morning? She did know one thing. If she ever wanted to work in Golden again she had better come clean to Mr. Morley. Sooner or later they were both going to find out who had performed this miracle, and she knew it hadn't been any one she knew. Confusion gripped her. What the heck was going on?

"Actually, six out of my seven men are sick with the flu, Mr. Morley. The seventh has a stomach bug."

Then Rebecca saw her room chart—on the small

table next to the fireplace. Each time a room had been painted someone had signed off. But she couldn't read the signature. The person who signed had written it in illegibly.

Mr. Morley's smile practically beamed. "I just knew you wouldn't let me down, Ms. Evans. I knew you'd have a Plan B. But then you couldn't be a successful business owner and not have a Plan B in place, could you?"

For a brief moment she considered telling him a fib. That her people had painted into the night for him. Her guilty conscience barked at her. She couldn't take credit for her company finishing this job. After all, this was her business—her life, and she wouldn't put its reputation on the line, no matter what.

The words "I had nothing to do with any of this, Mr. Morley" danced around the edge of her tongue. If he'd given her a moment more, she would have spit them out.

"When I saw Mr. McGill's truck in the driveway," Mr. Morley continued, "well, it was pure genius and quick thinking on your part to call in the help of a local contractor. Think outside of the box and stay on your toes; those are the keys to success. And you certainly used them, Ms. Evans. You certainly used them."

She smiled at the beaming Morley and quickly turned around pretending to survey the finished product further. Tears stung her eyes.

Travis.

Rebecca turned to face Mr. Morley. "I'd like to think all business owners in Golden would pitch in and help one another when and if the occasion arose."

Mr. Morley nodded. "If not all, at least McPherson

& McGill Construction."

Rebecca sighed. Leave it to Travis. He had just accomplished in one day what it had taken some business owners years to do. He had gotten on Mr. Morley's good side. A side every business owner in town knew was the only place to be.

Rebecca flashed a smile. "We couldn't have you unprepared for your grand reopening could we, sir?"

"Fine, fine," Mr. Morley murmured. "And thank you, Ms. Evans. You are one smart businesswoman. You and that Mr. McGill are looking at many prosperous years of business in this community. I'll guarantee you that."

Rebecca bit back a tear. Although she had to admit, Morley's compliment would have meant more if she had earned it on her own. Even so, this time she was more than happy to share the praise with Travis. Pushing negative feelings aside, she scolded herself for being ungrateful.

What was wrong with her? Travis had helped her when she needed it. And his help had sealed this deal insuring her years of future business. For that she would be eternally grateful.

****

Back at Designs of Distinction, Rebecca slowly inched her way across the room, arms full of window treatments for Mr. Morley, when a deep-throated chuckle caused her to jump.

Travis leaned against the antique armoire with his hands behind his back and studied her. "Have you been working out?"

Rebecca desperately tried to balance everything in her arms. "Were you trying to give me a heart attack, again?" As Travis helped her pile the window treatments onto the workroom table, she demanded, "How long have you been standing there?"

"Not long."

She shot him a disapproving look, and moved her arms up and down to regain the circulation she'd lost from carrying such a heavy load.

"I was only here a few minutes."

"I didn't hear you come in. You should be a professional lurker, McGill. You've got silent walking down to a T."

He walked behind the armoire, and returned with a bouquet of white calla lilies. Her favorite. Travis maintained the boyish grin on his face as he leaned closer. "For you," he said and handed her the lush bouquet.

He had done so much for her with the Morley job, and now flowers? The gesture was so unnecessary she felt the tough façade she had put in place upon his entering the shop vanish. She dipped her nose into the calla lilies and breathed in their sweet fragrance.

Tempted to ask what had compelled him to do such a thing, she disregarded the thought when the bell above the shop door rang and three women entered. Rebecca excused herself for a moment to see if they needed assistance.

When she returned Travis asked, "Busy day?"

She sat in the chair behind her desk. "Mr. Morley wastes no time."

"Don't give him all the credit." Travis sat in the chair opposite her desk and leaned back. His long legs spread wide before him.

At the sound of his voice, Rebecca's stomach

clenched. You can do this she told herself. She wouldn't be able to pretend the kiss hadn't happened, but she could make it clear that it wouldn't happen again. Ever. If he could act as if nothing had happened between them then so could she.

She leaned forward. She had to at least thank him. Let him know she would never forget what he had done for her, for her business. "What you did—meant more to me than—"

Her eyes bore through to his soul. Helping her had been his pleasure. He was just sorry he hadn't known sooner. She squirmed in her seat. *Damn.* He'd hoped bringing her flowers would alleviate the tension always thick in the air when they were together. No such luck. She bit at her bottom lip a sure sign she was a nervous wreck. In an attempt to calm her he said. "It was no big deal. We're both business owners right?"

She smiled. All evidence of burden seemed to disappear. "I've been told once you get on Morley's good side, you're in. So now we're both in."

Travis glanced at the customers perusing her shop. "I should let you get back to business."

Watching him leave, Rebecca rubbed her hands up and down her arms. So that was it? He had helped her out of obligation? A large sense of disappointment she didn't expect washed over her causing her heart to sink slightly in her chest.

For the first time since he'd returned to Golden, she was sorry he had to leave.

****

On Monday afternoon, Travis stood in the middle of Elizabeth's completed bedroom, unable to believe the transformation that had taken place. Man, was he way off base when it came to knowing what a teenager wanted. Gone was the bright pink paint, childish furniture and stuffed animals that had once dressed the room. The walls had been freshly painted in celery green; a white ceiling fan with huge wicker blades had been installed; and the furniture Liz and Becca ordered now in place.

The beige carpet with thick pile added lushness. The bedspread, draperies, shams and throw pillows, all done in shades of celery green and violet, added femininity. The bulletin board, lamps with fringed shades and pictures Elizabeth had scattered throughout the room added personality as well as warmth.

Travis blew out a deep breath. If Becca did all this with just one room, he couldn't wait to see what she had planned for the rest of the house.

With all systems go, Elizabeth loving her new room and Travis thrilled with the finished product, Rebecca sat them both down. It was time to plan the next room.

At first they argued. Travis felt that the family room should be next. Elizabeth argued that the kitchen should be next. Like bookends, both of them, father and daughter, sat there with their arms crossed.

"What do you suggest?" Travis shot Becca a look that pleaded for sympathy.

He had always been overly competitive. She bit her lip and willed herself not to get involved. However, by the determination on both their faces she had to say something. If she didn't they would be here all night.

When push came to shove, Rebecca agreed with Elizabeth, explaining that the kitchen was often the room where everyone spent most of their time. Her simple explanation seemed enough to appease him. Thank God. She wasn't up for a battle of the wits.

Before beginning with even the smallest design ideas, she explained to both of them how the kitchen would be a complete mess over the next few weeks, between ripping out counters and cabinets and refinishing the pumpkin pine floor, neither of them would see a completed room for a time period that could encompass as long as six weeks. Depending on how quickly the materials were available and how fast the contractors worked. The kitchen would be inoperable.

Getting back to the business at hand, Travis assured Rebecca repeatedly that workers in his house would not be a problem. Still she had doubts and he had never been a patient man.

Although he had overseen many renovations from start to finish, he'd never lived in any of those houses as the renovations were actually being performed. A gutted kitchen to a perfectionist like Travis could be detrimental to his sanity.

Liz, on the other hand, had enough optimism and enthusiasm for the three of them. Rebecca watched Travis' face light up as Elizabeth bounced around the kitchen describing the fixtures and cabinets they had chosen and exactly where they would be placed upon delivery.

Unexpected warmth toward him spread through her. Standing there with his hands on his hips, a smile on his face, he looked exactly like the doting father he had so happily become. Rebecca couldn't help but find Elizabeth's excitement contagious. Travis had been right. Knee deep in work he was hardly around to help with choices, and Rebecca couldn't be more pleased.

There was, however, one thing he had insisted on—authenticity. And Rebecca had promised not to let him down. So when she located a woodworker who specialized in recreating cabinetry from the early 1900's, she spent hours designing Travis' kitchen. Oak cabinets, decorative chair-rail reminiscent of the period, a china cupboard built into the wall and pocket doors that led into and out of the formal dining room were all touches she knew he would love. She had other ideas up her sleeve for the rest of the house, but for now she concentrated on the kitchen.

Elizabeth had a lot of input. And it hadn't taken long for Rebecca to see that the teenager had quite an eye for color. To her surprise, Elizabeth had even begun talking about interior design as a possible future. Rebecca felt humbled. She never realized she could make such an impression on someone.

But then, Elizabeth wasn't just anyone. She was a young girl, who due to the death of her mother, had seemed to be growing up right before Rebecca's eyes. No wonder Travis enjoyed every moment with her. He knew better than anyone how fast time passed. In only two years, Elizabeth would be off to college.

Rebecca's heart tightened. She pushed all sadness aside. She would live in the moment and appreciate the teen's company. She'd deal with the college issue later.

When she had to.

Chapter Eleven

The next day, right on schedule, Elizabeth stopped in the shop. “I’d kill for a home cooked meal.”

Rebecca cringed. Living without the basic kitchen amenities was hard for anyone, even someone with as much enthusiasm as Elizabeth. And take-out food grew old. Fast.

Unfortunately, the kitchen project wouldn’t be finished for weeks. late next week. Decorative wood molding the contractor had ordered hadn’t arrived yet and the built-in cupboard in the eating area couldn’t be completed without it. Also, the stove she had requested was on back order.

“I mean the food at Kate’s is good, but I don’t think I can force down another burger no matter how hard I try.”

What teenager turned down a burger? Elizabeth really must have had her fill. Rebecca wished she could help. She really did. But aside from the diet entrees she nuked for herself each night, her cooking expertise was more than limited.

“I’m sorry, Liz. I’d have the two of you over—”

“You will? When?”

Rebecca sighed. “I can’t cook. Not really.”

Liz looked surprised. “Sure you can. Anyone can cook.”

Liz’s optimism enveloped Rebecca and made her

believe, if only momentarily, that she might be right. She thought a moment. After all, even she could read a cookbook. “Maybe.”

“So we’ll see you tomorrow night at six?” Elizabeth asked.

Rebecca nodded and smiled wearily. *Tomorrow? Six?* The sigh trapped in her chest deflated like a slow leak in a balloon. She didn’t mind that Liz knew she was an amateur cook, but Travis was another subject. She could live very well without him teasing her.

Liz grabbed her backpack and slipped out the door.

So, that was that. The decision had been made. Rebecca decided to cook such a fabulous dinner for the three of them that Travis would be speechless.

Grabbing her keys, she locked up the shop for the night. She needed Michelle. Besides being a pediatrician, she was also a marvelous cook. Michelle would know exactly what Rebecca should prepare and how she should attack the recipe.

But Michelle wasn’t available. She was scheduled to see patients all afternoon. The one thing she did manage to tell Rebecca when she popped her head out of the examination room for a fraction of a second was to go home and watch one of the food shows on cable TV, sure she would be able to find a suitable recipe to follow.

Without any other choice, Rebecca did just that. Presently a woman chef was preparing desserts. Since she had already decided to buy her dessert for tomorrow night, she walked into the kitchen to make a cup of coffee. Hey, she was cooking a full dinner. Dessert from a bakery would have to do.

“After the commercial,” the chef said, “we’ll return

with, Roberta, as she shows you how to transform pork chops from mundane to mouth-watering."

Rebecca stopped stirring her coffee. *Pork chops? What a great idea.* Even with her limited cooking skills she could handle pork chops.

She grabbed a pen and paper and over the next hour listened intently to Roberta as she explained how to prepare Moroccan pork chops, glazed carrots, garlic mashed potatoes and a tossed salad with homemade vinaigrette dressing.

Clicking off the television, Rebecca smiled. Oh yes, she'd knock them out with her homemade meal. Placing the recipes on the coffee table she sighed as insecurity rushed through her. Why was she so nervous? This was Travis and Elizabeth. Why was she so worried about impressing *them*? After all they'd been eating take-out and Kate's food for almost three weeks. Anything she conjured up had to be better.

Confidence burst through her system. She glanced at her watch. The grocery store was open for a few more hours. If she hurried, she could get all her ingredients tonight. Rebecca grabbed her keys and purse and headed out the door.

****

Wednesday evening, right on time, Travis arrived at Becca's second-floor condo in a brick colonial in the center of town. Travis suspected she had chosen it for its close proximity to her shop, only six or so blocks away. However, when he entered, he suspected her choice to live here might have been based on stronger factors.

When he rang the bell loud growling emanated from the apartment. That couldn't be coming from the dog she'd shown him the picture of, could it? If he hadn't seen the picture, he would've assumed from the growling that the dog on the other side of the door was huge with ferocious teeth bared and ready to take a large bite out of him.

He took a step back.

When the door swung open, he wasn't prepared for the little black dog to bolt at the sight of him. He was everything but ferocious. Travis lifted his foot, damp from the too happy dog.

Becca pulled the animal back by his collar and with a stern tone said, "Sherlock, that's very bad." The dog cowered behind her.

Travis shook out his foot. "It's okay, I think he only got my shoe."

"Come in and I'll get you a towel to dry off."

He stepped inside and forgot all about his wet foot.

The inside of Becca's place was something out of a decorating magazine without being cold and sterile.

"I'll be right back," she promised.

The entry hall was larger than he expected. A black round wrought-iron table with fresh flowers sat in the center. Pale yellow paint dressed the walls and black wrought-iron sconces decorated the wall.

"Here." She handed him a small towel. "Wipe your foot. Are you sure he didn't get your slacks wet? He's a little older and gets overly excited. His last owner had very few visitors."

Travis dried his foot. "Positive. See? No harm done."

"Good. Come on in." He followed her into the warm and inviting kitchen. Black granite with small speckles of white and silver dressed the counter tops.

Maple cabinets adorned the walls. Smoked glass and black wrought-iron fixtures hung over the countertop and above the round glass kitchen table supported by an ornate black wrought-iron base.

The kitchen's ten foot tall ceiling gave the illusion that it went on forever, making the room feel large and open. The floor was dressed in beautiful terra cotta tile. All the appliances were black except for the refrigerator, which was stainless steel. Yes, everything had been tastefully chosen.

Travis watched Becca hand Sherlock a treat. The dog scampered happily into the living room. He took a closer look around, then stood back and laughed.

Rebecca stood behind the counter chopping tomatoes for the salad she was preparing. Her face a blank canvas. "What?"

"You're still a neat freak."

"Huh?"

There was nothing on the counter tops. Not even a cookie jar. "Tell me, do you still sort the clothes in your closet according to color?"

Rebecca blew out a loud breath. "You had me worried." She placed the tomato wedges into the salad bowl and wiped her hands on her apron.

"Why?"

"I thought you were going to say you disliked everything."

He shook his head. "Never. I love it. It's you."

"It was nothing but a gutted shell when I first walked through. I think the owner was overwhelmed with completing it, worried that he might not do it justice, you know?"

Travis nodded.

"Once I told him I was an interior designer, he seemed to relax." She opened a package of croutons and sprinkled them over the salad.

"Sounds like a nice guy."

"He was. He said he wasn't talented when it came to decorating. He used to live downstairs until his wife became ill and they moved to Florida. Now his nephew's family lives there. Good neighbors, quiet and considerate." The smile on her face told Travis she was proud of the outcome.

"The floor is beautiful."

"It's imported. From Mexico."

"Leave it to a designer."

Rebecca's laugh came from deep down in her belly and Travis had to do everything to stop from reaching over and pushing a stray hair behind her ear. He longed to touch her.

Walking over to the sink with the cutting board she ran the water. "No matter what changes I made, it would look better than before it was gutted."

"A woman with a plan."

"You could say that. It took time, but I finally have it the way I like it." After rinsing off the cutting board, she placed it in the dish drain to dry.

"How long?"

"Well, I knew I couldn't complete the project all at once, I didn't have the money. But that was okay, I did it one room at a time, except for the flooring. I'd had my eye on this tile for a year. So I ordered it and had it installed as soon as the papers were signed. I knew I didn't want to walk around on an unfinished floor."

"Smart move."

"Slowly I started with the essentials, bathroom,

kitchen etc."

"How long did everything take?"

She frowned. "Eighteen of the longest months of my life. Would you like a glass of wine?"

"Absolutely." Travis grimaced at her previous comment. "Now I understand why you were adamant about the time factor of our project to Liz and me."

Rebecca nodded. "Speaking of Elizabeth, where is she? She didn't stop in at the shop today. I hoped she wasn't sick." She reached into her beverage fridge and pulled out a bottle of white wine. "Would you prefer red?"

Travis shook his head. "White is fine." Becca couldn't drink red wine for as long as he'd known her, because nitrates gave her migraines.

"I'm sorry she isn't here."

"Don't worry about it. Miss Socialite is over at her friend Ali's, studying for a biology quiz. Afterward, she's sleeping over, and taking the bus to school in the morning from there."

"Ah yes, her best friend, Ali. Good for Elizabeth. Making friends is so important at her age."

Travis nodded. "Ali is a nice kid, her parents,too."

"Things are going well for the two of you then?"

Travis knew Liz told Becca everything that went on between them at home. Still, he couldn't help but be touched by her concern. "Now that she has the proper hangers for her clothes they are."

"Hangers?"

"It's a long story." He sat on a stool opposite her so he could watch her cook. When she turned to place the bottle on the counter behind her, he couldn't help notice she was wearing a pair of pointy high heels. *Damn.* She looked good in anything she wore. He couldn't help think she looked great in everything that was underneath too.

Becca prepared Moroccan baby pork chops, glazed carrots, garlic mashed potatoes, and a tossed salad with homemade vinaigrette dressing.

In an effort to get his mind off her curvaceous figure and avoid the embarrassment of being caught staring, he said, "So where did you learn to cook?"

Rebecca opened the broiler and turned the pork chops. "Television." She placed the fork on the spoon rest and covered the cooked carrots with foil. "What's so funny?"

His laugh was husky and low. "That's where I learned. I'm surprised Liz hasn't bragged about my culinary skills by now."

Rebecca smiled. "She has mentioned you make one mean marinara sauce."

He shook his head. "Leave it to a kid to only remember spaghetti sauce."

She held out a wooden spoon filled with salad greens she had just tossed for him to taste. As if he had radar, Sherlock appeared by her feet and growled up at Travis.

"Shhh," Rebecca ordered. "Go inside."

The dog slunk into the other room.

"Sorry, he's very protective of me."

When Travis' tongue flicked over his lips, her knees went a little weak.

"What is this dressing? It's delicious." He took the spoon from her hand and ate the remainder.

When he licked his fingers, she groaned inwardly.

"Homemade vinaigrette," she answered weakly.

Travis handed her the wooden spoon and the tips of their fingers touched. Hers tingled. Now more than ever, she knew whatever barrier she had thought she put between them no longer existed.

God help her.

****

He enjoyed watching Becca prepare dinner—such an old-fashioned task for a modern woman.

When she removed the pork chops from the broiler, they were golden brown. The pears she sliced and placed on top of the pork chops had caramelized with the brown sugar she added as a finishing touch.

Travis heard Rebecca's stomach growl. *Loudly.*

He couldn't help but laugh.

"I skipped lunch," she said apologetically. She measured Sherlock's kibble, placed it in the dog bowl and whistled. The black Scotty ambled over and sniffed at the bowl. Then he shot her a sad look.

"You can not have pork chops. This is your food. Eat."

After Sherlock snorted and retreated to his bed in the other room, Becca said, "His former owner spoiled him. The vet said he needs to drop a few pounds, so he's on a diet."

"I'm glad you have him. He sounds fierce from outside."

"Does he? Good. A little protection never hurt anyone."

They walked over to the table where she placed the platter with the pork chops then walked back outside. Travis carried over the carrots. After he sat, she joined him with the bottle of wine and the dish containing garlic mashed potatoes.

"Why do you do that?"

"Do what?"

"Skip meals?"

"I don't usually, but there are days I get so busy I lose track of the time. I raced back today to walk Sherlock and by the time I returned at the shop the phone didn't stop. Hey, did Liz speak to you about her walking him?"

"Yes, she did. I think it would be good for her. Thanks for asking."

"I'm thrilled she can help."

They passed everything around until each one had a plateful, then they began to eat. Travis broke the silence. "This is delicious. Cook for me like this every night and I'll be your slave."

He watched her swallow. Hard. Then he changed the subject. "I'm grateful for cable TV shows. I'm also glad I discovered it before Liz came to live with me. Otherwise the poor kid would be living on pizza and macaroni and cheese."

Rebecca laughed and wiped her mouth with her ivory linen napkin. "She did mention she was tired of hamburgers."

"When the kitchen is finished we'll have to have you over. This really is top notch. Too bad Liz had to miss it."

"I'd love to come to dinner." *Had she just said that? Out loud?* She changed the subject. "I would have loved her to be here too. But I'm happy that she's acclimated and has so many new friends."

"I'm even more thrilled that she's friends with you. You don't know how comforting it is to know she stops in to see you after school." He looked up and met

Rebecca's eyes. "Having another woman to talk with is priceless to her right now.

Rebecca smiled.

He was quiet for a moment. "It took a while for Liz to feel as though she fit in, but once she did, the other kids accepted her and now it's as though she's always lived here."

He sipped his wine. "She's everything to me—nothing like me, but everything to me." He cut into his pork chop. "She still misses her mom. But then I guess she always will."

Rebecca nodded. A mother's love couldn't be replaced. No matter how much a person wanted.

"Losing Bridgett was hard for her. They were very close. If I showed you pictures, you wouldn't believe how much Liz looks just like Bridgett."

Rebecca shook her head. "I don't need pictures."

"What do you mean?"

"Liz may look like her mom, but she's you, Travis." She put her fork down and grinned at him. "Her nose, her cheekbones, the way she stands with her hands on her hips when she's angry, her stubborn streak." Rebecca laughed. "Your daughter is one-hundred percent you."

His eyes grew wide. "I'll be damned."

She couldn't help smiling at the pride displayed on his face. Like a rooster ready to crow, he couldn't have stuck his chest out any more if he tried. She could tell it meant the world to him that he and his daughter shared commonalities. And she was more than thrilled that she had been the one to point them out to him.

After dinner, they cleared away the dishes and straightened up the kitchen. After she put a pot of coffee on to brew, they went into the living room where she switched the gas fireplace on. Its bright glow lit up the entire room.

Sherlock remained in his overstuffed dog bed but didn't take his eyes off Travis.

Rebecca sank into her large chenille sectional and sat gazing into the fire. Quite a few minutes passed before either of them spoke. They discussed the weather, Travis' renovation, Liz. Everything but the kiss they shared on the street the other day. She slipped into the kitchen and returned with a tray containing coffee and dessert.

Travis eyes lit up when he saw the chocolate cream pie on the tray. "You didn't?"

Rebecca shrugged and placed the tray on the coffee table. "I know I tend to spoil her too."

He reached over and touched her hand. "Forget about Liz, chocolate cream pie is my favorite too."

How could she have forgotten? All the times they had gone to the movies had been followed by a trip to Kate's for dessert. And Travis had always had the chocolate cream pie. "No biggie. I'll wrap her a huge piece and you can take it home with you."

"She'd love that. If she gets to it before I do."

"Fine. I'll send you home with two large slices. Sound better?"

"Umm-hum."

After finishing his cup of coffee, he used the fact that he had had a long day to head home. He had no control when it came to Becca. Staying could only lead to one thing. And she wasn't ready.

Rebecca handed him a plastic container with the chocolate cream pie she'd promised.

At the door he took one finger and moved her chin to face him. "I had a great time."

"Me, too." Her breath caught in her throat. He was going to kiss her. "I wasn't going to allow this to happen again."

Neither was he, but the electricity between them was too big for even him to ignore. "Don't fight fate." He covered her lips with his.

Excitement radiated through her and she reached up and ran her fingers through his soft wavy hair. Travis deepened the kiss and a moment later it was over. He slipped out and closed the door behind him.

She had let him kiss her. Again. Only this time she was okay with it. In fact, if he had leaned in for another, she wouldn't have denied him. Hearing him talk over dinner about Elizabeth, and seeing how his love for her had deepened within the short time she had been living with him, touched her.

Travis had gone from a single parent who only needed to worry about himself to a full-time father looking after a teenage girl who depended on him for everything. He had shown patience, love, concern, and discipline. He had grown up.

Tonight she gained a view of the man who had done a three sixty to accommodate his daughter's needs and Rebecca couldn't help but be impressed. Travis McGill had changed. And she more than liked the man he had become.

Chapter Twelve

Once home, Travis placed his keys on the oak table in the foyer. Hearing the television he walked into the living room. "Liz?"

The teenager sat on the sofa, bowl of popcorn in her lap. "How did it go?"

He shook his head. "What are you doing home?"

Liz pointed the remote at the television and lowered the sound. "Ali didn't feel good, so her mom drove me home."

"That was nice of her, but you could have called me."

"And interrupt you and Rebecca? No way. I can still go to Ali's sweet sixteen next weekend, right? 'Cause I can't wait. It's going to be way out of control."

Travis knew Liz had watched that show about super sweet sixteen parties on cable TV but he hadn't really taken it seriously. Even she laughed at the way the girls went overboard planning parties. What he hadn't known was that real girls, everyday girls, got into it, too.

"Out of control how?"

"Relax. Her parents will be there." Liz turned to face him as he sat on the sofa next to her. "I mean she's going to make this grand entrance and her parents are actually giving her a new car!"

"And you thought that was a flamboyant gift?"

Her mouth dropped open. “It’s a freaking Mercedes Benz, Dad.”

“Wow.” Travis swallowed hard. He had thought about getting Liz a car for her birthday, as well. But a Benz? Now that was never an option.

“Yeah, wow. I mean don’t get me wrong. To each his own.” The young girl tossed a kernel of popcorn into her mouth and sighed. “When I can afford a car, I want one of those small jeeps.”

He named a few medium-priced vehicles.

“Yeah, one of those.”

Travis smiled at her. He was a lucky man. She didn’t demand expensive gifts. Heck, she didn’t demand anything. Bridgett had done a wonderful job bringing up their daughter.

“So, how did it go with Rebecca?” Her enthusiasm piqued his interest.

“It was dinner with a friend. That’s all.”

Sure, it had been more. And it had ended with a kiss he could still feel on his lips, but he wasn’t about to tell her that. “Becca wished you could have made it.”

“Believe me, next time I have a choice between studying and being with you and Rebecca, you win.”

“Liz…”

“I know. School comes first.” She rolled her eyes in a way that told him she was teasing.

He stood and slipped out of his jacket. “Clean up and turn out the lights before you head upstairs.”

“Dad?”

He met her eyes.

“So the two of you had a nice time?”

“Of course.”

A smile like that of a Cheshire cat lit up his

daughter's beautiful face. "Why?"

She shrugged. "No reason."

Travis turned toward the stairs. Somehow he couldn't shake the idea that his daughter tried to play matchmaker tonight.

The next morning Travis placed a call to Rebecca. "I have to fly to Atlanta tomorrow and close a deal. I have no choice but to stay overnight. Could you spend the night with Liz at our place?" Sitting with his feet up on his desk, Travis held his breath as he waited for her answer. He hoped his voice didn't give away his nervousness.

Rebecca didn't answer right away and her hesitation caused him alarm. Had the kiss they shared last night been too much for her? When would he learn to constrain himself when it came to all matters involving her? He licked his lips that still tingled from where hers had been hours before. *Great.* More than likely he had botched things up between them again.

When he heard her laugh, Travis relaxed. Who was he kidding? She had felt the heat between them just as much as he. And she hadn't exactly pulled away. Kissing aside, she would do anything for Liz. The two of them shared a special bond. And for their special relationship and the way it kept growing, he could never repay her. He was grateful Liz confided in her and trusted her. No matter how close he and his daughter became, he could never give Liz what Becca did—that female connection so important to a young girl.

"I'd love to."

He blew out a deep breath. "Great. Help yourself to anything." Travis would love nothing more than to return to the fragrance of Becca on his sheets.

The vision of her soaking in his whirlpool tub raced through his head, instantly tightening his lower region. *Christ, what she did to him with only one thought.*

****

Friday night, Rebecca and Liz played board games, ordered pizza and watched movies until after midnight. Walking into the kitchen with her hands full of glasses for the dishwasher, Rebecca sighed. She was amazed by how at home she felt at Travis' place.

After saying goodnight to Elizabeth, Rebecca walked down the hall toward the guest room she planned to occupy. Passing Travis' room, she gently pushed the slightly ajar door open and entered his private domain.

His aftershave enveloped her. She breathed in the musky aroma and hugged herself. After all these years he still wore the same cologne. A black and white check custom bedspread adorned his king size bed and mahogany wood tones dressed the furniture. She'd done a good job in here, if she didn't say so herself.

Still she wished he'd listened to her when it came to his seating choice. Looking around the room she still thought he should have let her put the chaise lounge, upholstered in black brocade, against the opposite wall from the bed.

With the reading lamp he had chosen, it would have been the perfect finishing touch. But Travis had argued that chaise lounges were for girls no matter what they were upholstered in and instead opted for a large chair and ottoman. And even though the oversized chair suited him, she had hoped he'd splurge and get the chaise lounge anyway. His only concern was his daughter and putting his needs second. Rebecca found that trait to be very attractive.

Walking to his closet she swung the double doors open. Crisp, dry cleaned shirts and more than a dozen suits hung inside. From the mirror behind the door, Rebecca spied one of his already worn shirts hanging on a hook.

He must have forgotten to toss it in the laundry basket. She pulled the soft cotton shirt close and inhaled. Musky and male—it emanated his cologne instantly transporting her to a happier time. A time when she would have bet money the two of them would marry, a time when she had planned their future together down to their children's names.

Without another thought, she shed everything but her panties and slipped into his shirt. After folding her own clothes, she walked toward his king size bed and ran her hand over the bedspread. She felt naughty.

She had fantasized sleeping here dozens of times. With Travis. She patted the bed. Oh, what the heck. He wouldn't be home until tomorrow afternoon. He'd never know she had indulged. She rolled the spread and comforter down and crawled underneath. Burgundy flannel sheets embraced her.

Scrumptious.

A moment later she pulled a pillow toward her chest and fell fast asleep.

****

Travis was pissed.

His client's assistant had supplied him with incorrect information. The president of the company he had flown out to meet with hadn't been in Atlanta at all.

While he flew out there, the other man had flown to California. Hence, his trip to Atlanta had been a complete waste of time.

So he hailed a cab, returned to the airport, and took the next available flight home. Now, all he wanted was to climb into his own bed and get some sleep. But that wouldn't be as easy as he thought because when he walked into his bedroom, there was an angel asleep in his bed.

Travis rubbed his eyes. "Becca?"

She didn't move. He walked into his closet and spotted her clothes in a neat little pile. He took a deep breath and tried to remind himself he wasn't supposed to have returned until late tomorrow afternoon. He processed his options.

What would she think if she woke and found him here? He hoped she would be glad. After all, she was sleeping in his bed, wearing what appeared to be one of his shirts. Why was she so stubborn? Ever since he had returned to town she had done everything in her power to push him away. Seeing her now proved one thing; all her energy had been wasted. She wanted him.

After slipping into pajama bottoms he gently slid under the covers next to her. Travis figured as long as he didn't touch her that couldn't be wrong, could it?

He tucked a pillow under his head and lay on his back. Within minutes, she rolled against him.

She smelled fabulous.

Perhaps if he lay still and just concentrated on sleeping?

Her soft hand wrapped around his waist.

Okay. He'd have to move that.

She moaned.

When Travis tried to move her hand, she fussed. Instead, he rolled to face her and watched her sleep. She had grown more beautiful with the years. He reached over and brushed the back of his hand lightly against her cheek.

Every ounce of common sense urged him to roll onto his back and go to sleep. But this was Becca. Irresistible. Also the woman of his dreams.

Donning his shirt and crawling into his bed must have meant one thing. She wanted him as much as he wanted her.

Travis brushed a strand of hair away from her eyes and kissed her lightly on the cheek.

He kissed her chin then he kissed her mouth.

She let out a small gasp.

He ran a finger down her throat. “Babe, it’s just me.” He ran his hand through her hair and kissed her again. Deep and warm.

She pulled away and smacked his arm. “What the hell do you think you’re doing?”

He smiled. “I could ask the same question.”

Dazed, she looked around. “I was sleeping.”

His eyes skimmed her bodice. “You look sensational in my shirt.”

She quickly pulled the sheet tighter around her.

Travis knew all she had on were panties and his shirt. Her other clothes were in his closet. He tried to lift the sheet and peek underneath.

“Stop it.” She swatted his hand. “Let me out of here.”

Rebecca tried to edge off the bed, but he pulled the sheet toward him so she couldn’t move without coming undone.

"Answer two questions for me and I promise to let you go."

When she avoided his eyes, He moved closer like a mountain lion on all fours and lifted her chin with one finger. "Why are you wearing my shirt?"

When she didn't answer, he prodded, "Well?"

"Okay. It smelled nice."

"And?"

"It reminded me of you." Her voice was barely a whisper. "Are you happy now?"

"Very." He pulled her tiny waist closer and slid her under him making sure she could feel how much he wanted her.

"I've wanted to hear you say that since I returned. Say it again?" His voice was low and husky. He planted small kisses on her earlobes.

"No." She giggled.

"Then I'll say it. I want to be near you." He nibbled her neck as he lifted himself up and pushed the sheet aside. He lowered himself back down and his hands gently grabbed her bottom. *She wore a thong.*

"I love being near you. I love the scent of you. I want to make love to you. Having you in my bed is something I've been wishing would happen ever since we met on Main Street." He stopped kissing her and pulled her face close with both hands. "Want to know another wish of mine?"

Rebecca nodded. All sense and what not to do slipped away. She had missed him so much.

He whispered, "Take off the shirt."

If that's what he wanted, how could she say no?

She dropped his shirt to the floor.

"Hurry, he whispered."

She loved seeing the urgency, the need on his face. The fact that she still had the power to bring this man to his knees excited her more than she realized. Her nipples hardened as he stroked them.

Travis leaned his head back and bit his lip.

She smiled down at him. Why not make him wait? Just a little? She walked to the bottom of the bed and tossed her thong to the floor then she took her hair out of the ponytail she had pulled her hair into. Her wavy red hair cascaded onto her shoulders. She arched her back and shook out her hair.

He reached for her, but she backed away. Pushing her hair back and stretching her assets in front of him had been an even better tease.

"Becca," he begged.

See?

She straddled him with her legs and untied the drawstring on his pajama bottoms. His need for her pressed against the waistband.

She slipped her hand inside and palmed him. "All for me?" She chuckled. Every alarm in her body was going off, but Rebecca ignored them. This man was hard and hot for her and she wanted him.

Here and now.

She was enjoying herself too much to stop. Indulging in a fantasy she'd had for years was finally a reality and brought her to a level of excitement she couldn't control. There was no stopping now.

He pulled her softly down on top of him. "Tonight and every night," he whispered.

He kissed her neck and a moment later he was on top of her. He suckled her breasts, teasing, taunting first one, then the other. When his head slid down her stomach, she gasped. And when he parted her wetness and slipped his tongue inside her, she knew she had lost more than her physical self to Travis. She had lost her heart as well.

Running her hands through his hair, she pulled his head closer. When her back arched in response to the wonderful sensations he sent through her, he surprised her and changed strategies. When he slid two fingers inside, she sucked in as much air as possible. "Oh please, don't stop." So much for her being the one in control. She grasped the sheets and closed her eyes.

Travis whispered, "I love how you taste."

"And I love how you taste me," she groaned. And she loved the sensation he sent coursing through her. In response, her torso moved to his rhythmic strokes slowly, then building to a pace that nearly sent her flying through the air in pieces.

Travis increased his tongue thrusts until she swore she was about to come. When he withdrew for a moment to sheath himself she gazed at the length and thickness of him. She knew her eyes begged him to hurry, but she didn't care. There was no embarrassment between them. There never had been. Only years of want needing to escape.

He slipped back inside of her and she wrapped her legs tightly around him. Moving slowly with him at first he dropped small kisses on her neck. The full length of him dove deeper inside her. He thrust a final time and found oblivion. Rebecca called his name. *It was so right, so good.*

So Travis.

As she fell over the edge, he suckled her breasts. Her nipples hard and needy for attention.

"Ready for more?"

She heard herself purr like a kitten.

Gently he rolled her onto her stomach and propped a pillow under her tummy.

Gripping her buttocks, Travis moved slowly at first. He wasn't in a rush. Tonight was all about Becca. He wanted to please her, spend all night making love to her if that's what it took to make her understand how much he loved her.

He slipped his hands around to her breasts as she arched her back and thrust into her faster, harder—every instinct telling him he wouldn't be able to hold back much longer. A flash of light took his breath away and he shuddered. "Becca."

Chapter Thirteen

Morning peeked in as light streamed through the vertical blinds that dressed Travis' bedroom windows. Rebecca woke with his arm still wrapped protectively around her waist, his breathing deep and soft in her ear. Their lovemaking had gone late into the night and Rebecca had found Travis' ability to please her both overwhelming as well as satisfying. She wanted to close her eyes and return to last night.

Especially now with panic racing through her each moment she lie awake in his arms. All pleasure aside, last night had been a mistake. Not only had she and Travis gone too far, but she had done something even worse—she had fallen back in love with him.

Rebecca inched out from under Travis' arm. As if the young girl hadn't had enough to deal with lately, the last thing she wanted was Elizabeth to find her and Travis together. In bed. Or with the knowledge that they had spent the night together.

A teenage girl believed in happily ever after, and Rebecca knew false hope never led to anything but hurt. She cared for Elizabeth too much to promise her something that would never be. A union between her and Travis.

A chill traveled up her spine.

"Becca?"

She turned to face him. Even with bed head he was

sexy. She reached for the sheet.

Travis stopped her. He ran his hand gently over her breast. "You can't possibly tell me you're feeling shy." With one touch he had caused the liquid heat between her legs to awaken.

He had her right where he wanted, and to her dismay right where she wanted to be. "Especially after last night."

It took all of her strength to push his hand away. Trying to stand up her legs felt like noodles. They certainly had worked out last night.

"Elizabeth. We can't let her find us like this. What will she think?"

Travis stretched and rolled onto his back.

Rebecca couldn't stop gazing at his chest. She didn't remember him being so hairy.

He chuckled when he caught her staring.

"I'm glad you think this is funny," she spat.

"No. You're right. I think."

"You think?"

He rolled to his side all the time watching Becca walk away. "You're beautiful, you know that?"

The heat in his eyes told her she'd better dress fast.

"I think you're jumping to assumptions. I bet Liz would love to see us together."

No. Last night had been about two people indulging in fantasies. And that was all. She was a grown woman who would deal with Travis and the feelings he caused swirling inside her. But Elizabeth was too young and going through too much right now, to deal with the possibility of it not working out between two people she loved.

She caught the glint in his eye. He patted the empty

spot next to him and nodded toward his hand.

"No. Last night was bad."

Travis looked up at the ceiling. "That's not how I remember it. I think we were pretty damn good."

She picked a throw pillow up off the floor and threw it at him. "Would you be serious? That's not what I meant and you know it."

He laughed then walked over to where she stood in the closet searching for her clothes. He dangled her thong from his index finger. "Looking for this?"

Rebecca swatted the air in front of him. "Give that to me."

Travis wrapped his hands around her tiny waist and pulled her close. His lips captured hers and his hands swept the perimeter of her body, reminding Rebecca just how good they had been together. Like the flick of a switch her body turned to jelly under his touch. Travis lifted her up and carried her back to his bed.

"No. We can't," Rebecca persisted. Why was it when he acted so tender and warm she felt like a puppet in his arms willing to do his bidding?

"Oh, but I can," he whispered, wasting no time discarding the shirt she had yet to button.

The desire in his eyes was so thick she almost melted. Reality quickly snapped her back to the present. "Travis. Elizabeth, remember?"

His head was buried in her neck and if she let him have his way in another moment he would be back inside her. Rebecca held her breath and pushed him away.

"No."

Though a groan slipped from his throat, he persisted in nibbling on her neck. "She never comes in without knocking."

Rebecca pushed him off her.

Deflated, Travis sat on the edge of the bed, and ran his hand through his hair.

Rebecca slipped into her thong, then her jeans, then sat beside him. "I don't care if she knocks. I don't want her finding us together."

"You're being ridiculous."

"Is that right?"

Travis cupped her chin with one hand and kissed her. The words flew from his mouth. "Move in."

"What?"

He couldn't help himself. He wanted her with him every night. The confusion on her face said it all. When would he learn to take it slow? In an attempt to make the irrational statement he had just hit her with sound somewhat logical, he said, "If we tell Liz you're moving in, this will be easier for her to accept. Don't you think?"

"No. Moving in would only confuse her." *Not to mention me.* Moving in wouldn't solve anything. He could call it quits any time he wished. Where was the comfort in that?

"I don't see it that way."

"You wouldn't."

"What's that supposed to mean?"

Rebecca blew out a deep breath and buttoned her shirt. "Moving in would only benefit you."

"Not true. You would also benefit. Or was it just my imagination? Didn't you enjoy last night as much as I did?"

Rebecca sighed. How could she tell him that last night had changed her? That she'd fallen in love with him all over again? She couldn't and he'd never understand why. He was used to casual relationships. He would never commit.

"Answer me."

"Yes. Okay. I'm human too."

From the cocky grin that appeared on his face she knew last night had been an evening of great sex to Travis. That's all.

She pushed her feelings aside. Right now she felt like crying. "I think you're forgetting one important factor."

His face was blank.

She had to protect Elizabeth from being hurt. He was clueless. "Teenage girls are vulnerable and exceptionally impressionable. Not to mention sensitive. Elizabeth has gone through so much—"

"Damn." He ran his hand through his hair in disgust. "My daughter who is still healing from her mother's death is right down the hall and here I am acting like a teenager myself. I have to be the worst father in the world."

She sidled up beside him on the bed. "Stop it."

He met her eyes.

"You are not a bad father."

When she ran her hand down his cheek he stiffened. He couldn't help it. That was how much control she held over him. One touch and he was hard. But she was right. When it came to Liz, he had to be careful. So much had happened in her life over the past few weeks.

Travis slipped into his pajama bottoms then he came up behind her and wrapped his arms around her waist. His body reacted to the nearness of her. He pushed his needs aside.

Rebecca studied his handsome face—his eyes deep pools of brown chocolate. He leaned in to kiss her, but she moved away. Too many times in the past she had allowed his penetrating eyes and wonderful kisses to override her better judgment. Last night had been just another example.

She whispered, "This time there's more at stake than the two of us."

Still he couldn't help but think there had to be a way around this. And damn it, if there was, he'd figure it out. He wanted Rebecca in his life and in his bed.

"Let me do the worrying about Liz, okay?"

Sadness cloaked Rebecca's eyes. She pushed away from him. No matter what he said, she'd worry about Elizabeth forever. The young girl had entwined herself deep inside Rebecca's heart.

She forced a smile. "I have to go."

"Stay for breakfast."

"I can't." She headed for the door. Right now the last thing she needed was to look at Elizabeth across a breakfast table.

The kid could read her like a book. Besides she needed air. And time to think. Last night she had learned that her ability to resist Travis was gone. And Rebecca had never been more scared in her life.

"What should I tell Liz?

"You'll think of something," Rebecca assured him then slipped out the door.

****

Rebecca turned the key in her ignition and checked the time. Nine fifteen. She put the car in drive and headed toward Designs of Distinction. Since she had the rest of the afternoon free she would pick up a few files that needed work done and spend the rest of the afternoon catching up. Anything that would keep her mind off Travis.

A short while later, she pulled the car right in front of the shop. Main Street would be filled to the brim with cars and shoppers in another hour so she'd get in and get out fast.

She opened the shop door and walked toward her desk in the back. She took a few steps and stopped. Then she took a few more steps and stopped again. Was that someone talking in the stockroom? The hair on the back of her neck stood up. Was she being robbed? There were thousands of dollars worth of custom draperies in the stockroom as well as a sofa and various other items that could be sold for quite a few dollars.

She pulled out her cell phone and hit nine-one-one. The dispatcher picked up a moment later. "Nine-one-one what's your emergency?"

Rebecca whispered into the phone. "This is Rebecca Evans; I own Designs of Distinction, 543 Main Street, in Golden. I think there's a robber here."

"Are you in the shop now, ma'am?"

"Yes."

"Does the perpetrator know you're there?"

"I don't think so."

"Then please go outside and wait for the police. I've already summoned a squad car."

"Okay." Rebecca disconnected and turned toward the door. A second later she froze.

"Oh, Benjamin. You're so witty."

What the—?

Irate, embarrassed, confused, all of the above—

Rebecca stormed to the stockroom. What was her mother doing here? In the past she stopped in on occasion for some fringe, a pillow form or anything she needed for one of her do it yourself projects, but she usually left Rebecca a message advising her.

Irritation roiled. She'd almost had a heart attack thinking she was being robbed.

Laughter rippled from the stockroom and with each step Rebecca took she grew angrier. Flinging open the stockroom door she froze. Her mother and Benjamin were on her two thousand dollar down filled sofa, naked, doing—

Seeing Rebecca, Leigh grabbed the cashmere throw and covered herself. Benjamin didn't seem to care that they'd been caught doing the naughty. As a matter of fact the smile on his face was huge.

Her mother's voice on the other hand was absolutely shrill. "Rebecca, I..., that is we, didn't expect you so early." She jumped off the sofa and padded toward her.

No matter how hard she tried to run, she couldn't. Rebecca's feet were glued to the spot. She squeezed her eyes shut thinking it might dissolve what she'd just witnessed.

"Oh sweetheart. I'm sorry. I came in for some fringe and..."

Rebecca swallowed. "Got more than you were looking for, huh, Mom?"

"Sweetheart, I'm so sorry. We didn't come here with this idea in mind, it's just that one thing led to another and before you know it, well, I have absolutely no control with Benny."

"Benny?" Rebecca groaned.

At that moment two armed policemen burst into the shop. “Hands in the air.”

Leigh jumped and as she put her hands up, the throw went down.

Rebecca wished she could crawl under a rock.

The policemen just smiled ear to ear.

****

After Becca left, Travis got out of bed. There was no longer a need to stay there. She had left him restless with the scent of her shampoo lingering on his pillow, causing his groin to inadvertently tighten; and the need inside him, ready to scream. He turned on the shower. Instead of hot water, he turned the handle to cold. He’d need all the help he could get to keep thoughts of her at bay.

About forty minutes later he joined Liz in the kitchen. Coffee was brewing and she was making scrambled eggs and bacon.

“What’s this?” he asked, looking over her shoulder into the skillet.

She shrugged. “Breakfast.”

“Great,” he said. Looking at the kitchen table he saw she had set three place settings. Regret raced through him. Why couldn’t he have come home last night and slept in one of the guest rooms or even on the sofa? Then she would still be here. She had been all curled up in his bed, and simply irresistible, that’s why. Their night together was one he’d never forget. Why couldn’t things be easier?

He paused a moment trying to decide what to say about Becca and her quick departure. The sound of toast popping up brought him back to the problem at hand.

"When Becca comes out, we can eat."

So much for the inevitable. "I'm sorry, honey, she left."

Disappointment flanked the teen's face. "When?"

Travis hesitated. "I don't know, about forty minutes ago. She said she had a ton of work to do for tomorrow, so she slipped out. She didn't want to wake you."

"Well, I guess if she had to go."

"She would have stayed if she could, Liz, but like I said—"

"I know. She had work. Still, I wanted her to see that I can cook."

"And she would have loved it. I'm sure."

"She works too hard."

Travis nodded.

"Just like you."

She had him there.

"Do you think she'd like it if I brought over some muffins to her place in a little while?"

"Sure."

Travis felt terrible about her disappointment. He wanted to tell her it was his fault that she had left so quickly—his fault that he couldn't control himself, his fault he jumped to conclusions, and his fault she had left here confused and overwhelmed. Since explaining this would probably take him the better part of the morning, he pushed that option aside. Instead, he spent the next half hour enjoying the lovely breakfast Liz had prepared.

The look of contentment on his daughter's face spoke volumes. Helping her clear the table, he thanked her for cooking. He leaned down to accept the kiss on his cheek and the hug he so desperately needed right now. After placing the dishes in the dishwasher, Liz headed upstairs for a shower. Travis sat at the table and stared out at the snow-capped mountains in the distance.

Thoughts of the two of them together last night flooded his mind. Why couldn't their morning have ended on a better note? *Because you opened your big mouth before thinking, that's why.* His offer for her to move in had sent her running like a deer in pursuit. He wasn't stupid. He could feel the tension between them and see the apprehension in her eyes before she had slipped out the back door.

Irritation niggled at him. He should have stopped her. Apologized. But he hadn't. He'd just sat there and watched her leave, afraid his pleading might only push her further away.

****

"Elizabeth? What a nice surprise!"

Rebecca held the door open wide for her to enter as Sherlock jumped up, tail wagging like the propeller of a boat. Liz bent and scooped up the little dog she had become fast friends with since she'd started walking him every day for Rebecca. Sherlock covered her cheeks with kisses.

"I just got out of the shower." She fumbled with the towel holding her wet hair atop of her head. "That's better."

Elizabeth placed Sherlock on the floor and handed Rebecca a basket covered by a napkin. "You missed breakfast so I brought you these."

Peering under the napkin she said, "Muffins? I love muffins."

"I know."

That's right, she did. Along with her favorite color, flower, and just about anything else you could name. "Come into the kitchen, I just made some coffee. Will you join me?"

Elizabeth smiled and almost skipped alongside Rebecca, Sherlock right behind them. "Sure, there's always room for a muffin."

After pouring herself a mug of coffee, Rebecca placed two plates on the table and poured Elizabeth a glass of milk.

Elizabeth looked down at the dog that was scratching at her leg. "No. You can't have these. Sugar is bad for you." She walked to the counter and opened the canister with dog paws printed on it and pulled one of his treats out. "Sit."

When the dog began to spin around in canine anticipation, Liz said firmly, "No."

He stopped.

"Sit," she repeated.

Sherlock sat and tipped his little head in question.

"Good boy." Elizabeth bent and handed him his treat. The little dog grabbed it and sped over to his cushy bed in the corner of the room.

"Well, I'll be." Rebecca's eyes widened. "I've never been able to get him to listen to me."

Elizabeth shrugged. "We understand each other."

"Hey, whatever works." She bit into one of the muffins and moaned. "These are delicious." Moist and bursting with cranberries, the pungent taste of the fruit woke all of Rebecca's taste buds.

"Thanks, Mom used to make them for me all the time."

"I love the raisins and the cranberries."

"Me too."

The two of them sat quietly eating until Rebecca broke the silence. "What do you have planned for today?"

Elizabeth shrugged. "Not much."

Rebecca placed a piece of her muffin on the dish. "I'm sorry I didn't stay for breakfast."

"Dad said you had to get some work done."

"That's right." She hated lying to Elizabeth but right now there wasn't much of a choice. "But, if I'd known you were planning on cooking, I would have made time and stayed."

"I wanted to surprise the both of you."

The both of you. Rebecca fingered the gold initial R she wore around her neck that her parents had gotten her years ago. Poor kid had done something nice and she had disappointed her. Somehow she would make it up to her.

"You did. These muffins are a lovely surprise."

Elizabeth crossed her arms. "I like when you come over to our place. It feels—"

Rebecca reached over and touched the top of her hand. "What?"

The young girl smirked. "Normal." Then she nodded. "Yeah, normal." A moment later she added, "Not that living with Dad isn't normal. It's just nice to have another girl in the house. That's all."

Rebecca smiled. She didn't know how to respond. Elizabeth had grown up with her mom around twenty-four seven. Living with her dad was different and Rebecca couldn't help feel that there were things she kept from him.

Elizabeth put her half eaten muffin down. “Not any girl, just you.”

Rebecca nodded and let her continue.

“I mean I can tell you anything. Talk to you about anything. You feel that way too, don’t you?”

“Absolutely.” She pressed her lips together.

Elizabeth sighed and got right to the point. “Did you and Dad have a fight last night?”

“No. I was asleep when he got home.”

“Look I don’t expect you to talk about your sex life.”

Rebecca pulled at the collar of her blue and white striped button down.

“Are you upset that I know you stayed over?”

A flush creeped across her cheeks. “No. Of course not. You’re not a baby.”

“I can see that you don’t want to talk about this.”

“What makes you say that?” She swallowed hard then stuffed a bite muffin in her mouth.

“Well, for starters you’re all white. Do you feel okay?”

“Yes, yes. I’m fine.” Liar.

“It’s just that now that you and Dad have—you know, I figured you’d understand better.”

Rebecca washed her bite of muffin down with coffee. “Understand what?”

“I, I have a boyfriend.”

“You do? Since when?”

Elizabeth nodded. A large grin dressed her face.

“I met him when we moved here, and we’ve even been out a few times. It’s amazing how we clicked, you know?”

Unfortunately she did. But Rebecca couldn’t help

wondering how Travis would handle this news.

“Dad doesn’t know, please don’t say anything.”

“I wouldn’t,” Rebecca said. “That’s up to you.”

“Anyway, we’ve gotten very close. I really like him.”

“That’s great, honey.”

“I’m not so sure.”

“About your dad?”

Elizabeth’s eyebrows squeezed together.

“Your dad had to know sooner or later you would have a boyfriend.”

“I know. It’s not my father I’m concerned about. It’s Christian. Well, we’ve gotten very close. You know what I mean, right?”

Rebecca frowned. “Do I?”

“Well, we’ve made out and—other things.”

Oh, no. Rebecca wasn't ready for this.

“Well, he wants—” The teen’s hands almost curled into fists then she straightened them.

Rebecca struggled to find the right words that might guide Elizabeth, but came up with nothing. She hoped the boy wasn’t pressuring Elizabeth to do something she wasn’t ready for.

“I mean I love him, I really do. He’s everything. And he loves me, he’s told me. I just don’t know if I want to, you know?”

Rebecca sighed and tried to keep her voice light and non-confrontational. Young love. Puppy love, call it what you like but she would not be the one to tell Elizabeth this wasn’t real love. She would, however, try and protect her for as long as possible. “No one should force or pressure any one into doing anything they’re not ready for.”

"Right, like you and Dad."

Rebecca just couldn't get used to the way Elizabeth treated her and Travis being together now so nonchalantly.

"You were ready, so you slept together." Relief flooded Elizabeth's face. "That's how I feel about the whole thing. Two people should take their time and when they're ready then they move their relationship to the next level."

Rebecca's breath hitched in her chest. Oh no, was Elizabeth saying she wanted to sleep with Christian? At only fifteen? Please God, let me be wrong. "And Christian? How does he feel?" She tried to hide the tension flooding through her.

"He disagrees."

"He isn't pushing you, is he?"

"No. He thinks love is the only thing two people need to prove that they're ready to share in a physical relationship."

If it were only that easy. How could she tell her that testosterone was what made a man's decisions for him without sounding like she was preaching?

"But I think I'm right. I mean, it is my body."

"Absolutely." She let out a huge breath.

"I do love him, though."

"I know."

"And I don't want to lose him. I'm just not ready to do it."

"Then don't. Plain and simple."

Elizabeth rolled her eyes. "I know I sound weird saying this, but isn't a woman's virginity the most special thing she can give to a man? And shouldn't I be selective in who I choose to share that gift with when

I'm ready?"

Rebecca sat straight up in her chair. She was impressed with Elizabeth's honesty and her clear and focused thinking although she still hated all that the teen knew about their night together. "Yes, yes, absolutely. You're one smart kid."

"Mom and I talked about everything too." The young girl's eyes brimmed with tears.

Rebecca bit her bottom lip. "She was a smart woman. But honey, sometimes things happen that we don't plan to have happen, hormones, feelings, they get in the way of thinking rationally, and I'd hate to see you make a mistake that could change your life forever."

Elizabeth nodded then laughed loudly. "Don't worry Rebecca, Christian always carries condoms."

Bile rose in Rebecca's throat. She was so not ready for this discussion.

A few minutes later, Elizabeth stood and turned toward the door. "Thanks for the talk."

"Anytime, honey, anytime." At the door they hugged goodbye.

She closed the door behind Elizabeth and leaned against its heavy wood. Sherlock barked for attention. She scooped him up under her arm and walked toward the bathroom where he'd sit and watch her through the shower door.

Elizabeth was a clear and smart thinker. She just prayed Christian's conveniently being equipped with condoms didn't sway the teen from her testimonial of a few minutes ago. And Travis, well he hadn't gotten the gist of being a full-time father yet, and she knew there was no way in hell he'd handle a pregnant teenager without losing his mind.

Rebecca gave Elizabeth a lot of credit and conceded she could learn a lesson from the teen about self-control when it came to the opposite sex.

Who knew?

Chapter Fourteen

Later that night, a loud noise in the hall woke Travis from a deep sleep. He lay there and listened hard. There it was again. Since her room had been redecorated, Elizabeth had been sleeping like a log. Something must be wrong for her to be awake this late. He stumbled into the hall where he collided with his daughter. Her face was whiter than cotton.

"What's wrong?"

"I don't feel so good. Maybe I had too much popcorn at the movies today."

He felt her forehead. "You're hot."

"I think I'm going to be—" Liz gripped her abdomen and kneeled in the hall.

Travis tried to grab her before she went down, but it was too late. Liz vomited all over the hallway floor. Thank God she missed the area rug. That was one clean-up job he didn't want. When she finished he helped her into the bathroom. Holding her hair as she hunched over the toilet, ridding her stomach of any and all contents, Travis was glad to be there for her. Taking care of her was a task he never wanted to end.

When she was through, he handed her a small cup of cool water to rinse her mouth, but Liz wanted nothing to do with it. She was too weak and only wanted to rest. Yawning, she curled up in a ball and lay on the rug by the sink. She looked so tiny. And Travis felt so helpless. He reached down and felt her forehead again, her fever hadn't lessened. If he didn't know better it was getting worse. Or was she just hot from her ordeal?

"Come on, honey, if you're burning up. You should be in bed." He lifted her into his arms. She was as light as air. He headed toward her bedroom.

"No. Please," she whispered, leaning into his chest.

"Where do you want to go?"

"Can I stay in your room? I hate to be alone when I'm sick."

"Okay." Travis sighed. This was new to him. She'd never been ill before when she had come to stay with him. As a matter of fact, the last time he had been there for her when she had gotten sick she was only two. Confused and upset, she was too young to know what had been happening to her.

He placed her on his bed praying she didn't get sick there. After he gave her two aspirin tablets and some water, he watched her roll up under his flannel sheets and comforter. He didn't know what else to do for her, and was happy to see that for now, she seemed comfortable. For that he was grateful, because he felt absolutely helpless. Quietly, he walked to the bathroom for some towels to clean up the mess in the hall.

She must have sensed him leaving. "You're coming back, aren't you?"

Travis smiled. "I was going to sleep in one of the guest rooms."

"But I hate being alone when I'm sick."

He walked to his bed and eased her back down under the covers. If staying would make her feel better, then he'd stay—even if it meant sleeping on the floor.

“Just don’t leave me, okay?”

He nodded.

“You can sleep on that chair over there, can’t you?” She pointed to the large upholstered chair in the corner next to the reading lamp. He wished he had taken Becca’s advice and gotten that chaise lounge when they had decorated his room. He couldn’t sleep in the chair he’d insisted on. Read, yes, sleep? No. It didn’t have a high enough back to lean his head on. And even with the ottoman, his long legs would be cramped.

No. Tonight, the floor was definitely the best choice. So it was either sleep on the chair and have cramped legs in the morning, or sleep on the floor and have an achy back. Travis opted for an achy back.

“I'll be back after I clean up the hall. Try and sleep now, okay?”

“Okay,” she mumbled slipping back under the sheets. She was asleep before he left the room.

After cleaning up the hall he carried the dirty towels downstairs into the basement where they kept the washer and dryer. When he turned on the light, his eyes opened wide and he gulped. Hangers with dainty panties and bras hung neatly in a row on a make shift clothesline. The reality that his daughter was a young woman couldn’t have slapped him harder.

Note to self—stay out of here in the future. Clearly, she had claimed it as her territory. Since tonight’s circumstances had left him no choice, he quickly added detergent, started the machine and made a swift exit. He’d toss the towels in the dryer tomorrow. Right now, he wanted out of there.

The next morning Liz woke and jumped out of bed

and right onto Travis' back. He had made a makeshift bed with comforters from the closet and put it next to the side of his bed. Just in case she woke up and needed him. He wanted to make sure he heard her.

"Ow."

She looked down and saw him on the floor. "What are you doing?"

He grunted. "Sleeping."

She jumped off his back. "Down there?"

He stretched. He was getting too old for things like sleeping on floors.

"What happened to the chair?" she asked, offering a hand to help him up.

"It was too small for me to get comfortable; the floor was a better choice." He groaned from the pain that had just shot down his back. "I thought."

"I'm starving." She grinned. "Let's make pancakes." He watched her scurry out of his room and down to the kitchen.

"Right. Pancakes." He grunted. "Glad to see you're feeling chipper." He placed his hands on his lower back and leaned into a stretch. At least someone felt good.

****

Over the past three days Rebecca had worked extra hard to clear her desk of any outstanding projects that needed her attention. Lately she'd been feeling like all the fun she'd used to have as a designer had disappeared. In a rut, she needed to regroup. Recharge.

So she planned to drive into Philadelphia tomorrow morning to attend the Annual Decorator's Convention. It was only two days, but it would be just enough time to refuel, and she'd be headed back home by Thursday night.

Yes. Refueling her creative energy and returning with new and exciting design ideas was just what she needed. She hadn't attended last year's convention due to business obligations and had promised herself that nothing would keep her away this year.

The annual decorator's convention was a place to view all the new products available in home design. It was a decorator's chance to preview these items before the general public. And it was fun. There were new fabrics, tons of carpeting and new hard window treatments. It was also a place for decorators to meet other decorators and discuss the latest trends, products, and marketing strategies. Just thinking about attending the conference shot a jolt of excitement through her. No doubt about it, this little jaunt was just what she needed.

On a personal note, she couldn't deny that part of her decision had to do with avoiding Travis and their unresolved feelings. She convinced herself that escaping for a few days was a good idea. After all, her business was her only source of income. As one businessperson to another, Travis would more than understand.

****

That night after returning home late from work, Travis retrieved his briefcase from the trunk of his car and strode up the front walkway. The landscaper Becca had recommended had done beautiful work. When he'd bought the house the view of the old Victorian was blocked from the street with overgrown trees, shrubs and weeds of every species.

Now he was happy to say the home's curb appeal had increased ninety-nine percent. The walkway was created with red pavers, which met at the staircase and formed a huge circle. Liz had asked if they could put a wrought iron bench out front so she could sit and read. It had been a great idea. Two oak trees had been planted framing the house, along with rhododendrons, burning bushes, and evergreen shrubs. Yes, money was going out of his wallet faster than he could make it. Thank God the situation was temporary. Once he got the house the way he wanted, he would save again.

On a normal evening he would be able to enter the house through the garage, but since Liz still hadn't emptied all the boxes Cecile had forwarded from Chicago, his car had had to sit in the driveway. Over a dozen boxes had been forwarded last week. How much stuff did she own?

Travis stumbled over a rock on the pavement. *Damn.* Liz could at least have switched the outside lights on for him. Kids. Enough with the tomorrow I'll do it, dad. He'd have her address those boxes this week or he'd know why. And if she chose not to, the answer was simple. The remaining boxes would be stored in the attic. He wanted his car back in the garage. He hated exposing it to the elements.

Glancing at the face of the house, Travis noticed most of the lights inside were off. He figured Liz was either watching a movie or had gone to bed early. As he reached for his key to unlock the door, he hoped she was sleeping. It had been a lousy day, and he didn't feel like making small talk.

He didn't feel like talking at all. After trying to contact Becca unsuccessfully three times today, he couldn't stop visions of her beautiful body from floating into his mind and other parts of his anatomy. He had woken up Sunday morning more addicted to her than he had ever been. He just didn't see the problem. He'd bet anything she wanted him as much as he wanted her.

When Becca had left so abruptly, she wounded his ego not to mention leaving him horny as hell. *Christ, he was a thirty-six year old horny guy who had no chance of getting any. He was pathetic.* But then what had he expected? It was simple really. She wanted a commitment. And here he was all these years later, still unable to give her just that.

One marriage down the tubes and no guarantee another would last, sure he was scared, what guy wouldn't be? If only his divorce hadn't been such a bad experience. But it had and instead of being happily married, Travis had found himself alone and only allowed to see his daughter every other weekend or when her schedule permitted. It was no way for her to grow up, and no way for him to live.

Only now, Liz was no longer three years old. This time she was fifteen and old enough to be devastated by a break up. His break up with a woman Liz had come to care for. Becca meant the world to her, and to him.

Becca was smart. She sensed his apprehension before she slipped out of his house early. Asking her to move in had been an easy out. Why commit if she would meet him halfway and make it that much easier? He ran his hand through his hair in frustration. That had been lame of him. And if he could take it back he would. *When the hell would he learn to slow down, not rush things with her?*

Ever since his marriage ended, he hadn't been able to get close to another woman. Really close. Thinking about it now, it suddenly became clear. He had been dating the wrong women. *Woman.* No wonder none of them could meet his standards and his standard had always been Becca.

Now that she was back in his life, he found that she was all he wanted. He reminded himself to stop moving so fast. She wasn't up for it. Could he blame her? Anyone with feelings wouldn't have been able to forget his thoughtless departure from their life all those years ago. His inability to explain his departure and keep the promises they had made one another showed his weakness. He placed his keys on the table in the foyer then turned and walked toward the living room. When he switched on the lights, Travis knew one thing: If the blond haired punk who had just jumped off his daughter didn't get out of here within one minute—he might not live to see tomorrow.

Because he might just kill the kid.

Travis clenched his fists and pointed toward the door. He growled, "Out. Now."

The young man stammered, "Yes, sir."

Travis watched as the boy ran his hand through his hair and shot a look in Liz's direction. His big puppy dog eyes full of—what was that? Remorse? Was this kid serious?

Travis didn't care. He coughed. Loudly.

The kid swallowed hard and looked directly at him. "I'm very sorry, Mr. McGill. Please don't punish Liz. It was my fault."

Travis put his hands on his hips and moved closer to the boy. "Weren't you just leaving?"

"Yes, sir."

The boy shot by Travis, but not before he looked at Liz one last time.

Liz sat at the edge of the sofa. Her knees pulled up to her chest. A glazed expression coated her face.

He couldn't believe how irresponsible she had been. Sure he had worked late and left her alone. But this wasn't the first time. They had an agreement. She'd keep the doors locked and not allow anyone in. What was it about this boy that allowed her to break her word to Travis? He had no idea.

But he was done with reasoning—with trying to figure out what made her tick, what motivated her, and what hurt her. He had come to the end of his rope.

He was her father. He had no choice but to punish her. If he didn't set limits now, God knows what she'd do next.

He stood in front of her and started counting off fingers. "No stereo, no phone, house or cell, no TV, no computer unless it's for school."

"Please stop."

"No. I trusted you. Since when are you allowed guests when I'm not home?"

Liz's head spun around to meet his. "Who are you to talk about trust?"

Where the hell had that come from?

"What?"

"Rebecca can't trust you. Why should I? And now you preach trust to me?"

"This conversation is not about Becca and me. This is about *you*. You're only fifteen years old. And who are you to discuss *our* relationship? I don't mind you stopping by to talk to her, but now that I know you're discussing *me*, maybe you should stop going over there completely."

Elizabeth jumped off the couch. "No! You can't

stop me. She's my best friend. Besides, she doesn't talk about you. Ever. I do. I just assumed. Oh forget it. And don't tell me I can't talk to her anymore."

His daughter's eyes filled with tears.

Travis dropped his hands from his hips and walked toward her. He kept his voice low. "We can discuss Becca another time. Right now I want to talk about tonight and what I just walked in on."

"I'd rather not."

He ran his hand across his five o'clock shadow. He was so angry he could hit something. He had let her down. What the hell was wrong with him? Couldn't he come through for any of the women in his life?

"I can't believe I found you—"

She interrupted him, "Consoling a friend."

"Honey, the next time I need consoling, I hope some wonderful woman treats me the way you treated that boy."

"His name is Christian."

"Well, your lips and his were locked. And his hands—I can't talk about it without wanting to rip *Christian* in half."

She wiped away a tear.

Travis sat on the sofa and sighed. He opened his arms and she didn't hesitate to fold into them. Liz cried hard and gripped his shirt as though she'd never see him again.

Had he yelled that loud?

When she buried her face deeper into his chest and cried harder, he silently cursed himself. He leaned back and held her, feeling like the worst father in the world. And this conversation wasn't near being over yet.

She picked her head up and wiped her eyes. "His

mother died."

"What?"

Her bottom lip trembled, "Christian's mother. She died tonight at six o'clock. He didn't know where else to go, so he came here."

Travis pulled her close again and leaned back into the soft leather cushions. "Great. And I kicked him out. Where will he go now?"

She sniffled and lifted her head off his chest. "Home. His father and brothers are waiting for him. I made him call them when he got here."

"You did the right thing."

"We talked a lot, Dad." Her voice was barely audible. "Christian knows I just lost Mom. I hugged him, he hugged me, and the next thing I knew we were kissing."

"Things can get out of hand fast," Travis warned.

She nodded.

"You're too vulnerable for anyone to seek consoling from right now. Things could have escalated. Well, I don't even want to think about that."

She nodded again.

Travis knew he was asking a lot from her. After all, she was just a kid. A fifteen-year-old beautiful kid who had no idea dozens of guys would be banging down the door over the next few years for the chance to get into her pants.

Damn it. Work would never come first again. Never. "Bottom line is you shouldn't have let him in when I wasn't home."

She lifted her head and looked at him. "But he had nowhere else to go. Don't you think there's an exception to every rule?"

Travis leaned his head against the sofa and blew out a deep sigh. She had him there.

Her eyes bore a hole through his forehead. "Well?"

"Only in extreme cases."

Travis reached up and pushed a few strands of stray hair behind his daughter's ear. What was this? A second piercing in her ear? He moved the hair completely away from her face. A third piercing? Elizabeth now had three holes in each earlobe?

He touched her ear. "When did you get these?"

She bit her lower lip. "At the mall?"

He shook his head. "Why did you feel compelled to put additional holes in yourself?"

She got up and walked to the other side of the room and crossed her arms, obviously in shutdown mode.

"Well?"

"Rebecca said you would be mad."

Travis sighed. This was getting more complicated by the moment. "She knew about this?"

Liz nodded. "She wasn't with me, but I showed her afterward."

Why did every conversation they had keep going back to Becca? He ran his hand through his hair.

"I did it with some friends of mine last week. I meant to tell you, but I forgot."

"You forgot to tell me you have two additional holes in each ear?"

"Why do you have to make everything into such a big deal?"

His eyes grazed over her outfit. "Why do all your shirts not cover your belly button?"

"Dad?"

"Liz?"

They stood nose-to-nose and stared at each other neither one giving the other the satisfaction of backing down. A moment later, Travis smirked. "Becca was right."

She looked at him quizzically.

"She said you were just as stubborn as me."

Liz smiled up at him. "I'm sorry I didn't tell you sooner."

"How about you're sorry you didn't ask permission?" Travis sighed deeply. *He felt as though he'd aged ten years in the last five minutes.* "I guess I'll learn to live with the earrings. I can also live with the belly button thing." He pointed toward her shirt.

His daughter smiled at him. "Everyone wears their shirts like this."

Travis rolled his eyes. "Whatever."

Liz stared at him in amazement.

"What?"

"You just said *whatever*."

He changed the subject. "In the future, promise me you'll talk to me about any other alterations you're considering making." He drew a Z in front of his daughter's body with his finger like she always did when she wanted to make a point.

She laughed. "Please. Never do that again."

Travis grinned. "Fine. As long as you don't pierce anything else."

Chapter Fifteen

Wednesday afternoon, Liz wandered into the kitchen after a trip to the mall with her friends. “Where’s Rebecca?”

Standing there in front of him with her arms folded across her middle, Travis gaped at her right bicep. “What’s that?”

She rolled her eyes and walked to the refrigerator for a soda. “Relax.”

“Excuse me?”

She nodded. “The vein in your neck is pulsing.”

He clenched his fists in frustration. “Why would you do that to your beautiful arm?” He pointed to the tattoo of a hibiscus flower that had taken up residence on her arm.

The kid shrugged, not seeming the least bit concerned that she had just tainted her perfect body.

For life.

“It’s just a tattoo.”

His stomach churned. “I love your blasé attitude. But I disagree. A tattoo is forever. When you’re forty you’re going to hate yourself for having done this.” His eyes fixated on the tattoo, no matter how much he tried, he’d never understand a teenage girl’s mind and how it worked.

“You’re getting nuts over nothing.”

Travis’ stomach knotted. *When the hell had he lost*

complete control?

"Dad, are you okay? Your face is really white."

He sat at the kitchen table and nodded. "I think so."

"I didn't think you'd react this way."

"What? You thought I'd be happy?" Reality swooped in and Travis said, "Wait a minute, don't you have to be eighteen to have a tattoo applied?"

"Not a henna tattoo."

A temporary tattoo. Relief washed over him as he snapped, "Don't ever do that to me again."

"I was just teasing. I'd never get a permanent tattoo on my arm."

"Thank God."

"Maybe my lower back, or one around my waist that looks like a chain belt? They're so cool."

Travis' legs weakened. *God help him.*

"Relax, Dad, it's not like I went and got a real one. Yet," Liz said before hugging him.

Travis didn't think he'd ever truly relax again, not as long as he had his free-spirited daughter living under his roof, piercing assorted parts of her body, and contemplating various tattoos.

"So where is Rebecca?"

Her question snapped him out of his fixation with her arm. Come to think of it, he had been wondering the same thing. Becca hadn't returned any of his calls. He assumed that was her way of keeping her distance between them. And he wasn't about to push her further away. So, after the third message he stopped calling. He could take a hint. He would give her as much time as she needed. "I'm not sure."

Liz's mouth dropped open. She shot him a look of confusion. "How can you not know? You're her boyfriend, aren't you?"

It was as though they had switched roles. She the parent; he the child. He ran his hand roughly through his hair.

He couldn't answer her because he wasn't sure what to say. He wanted to say, yes, hell, she's mine. But he stopped himself. After all, Becca was avoiding him. And he had no one to blame but himself.

"I stopped by her shop before I came home. It was closed," she said. "Yesterday, too."

Travis had asked Michelle yesterday, and all she would say was that Becca was out of town on business. Knowing the two of them were as thick as thieves, Travis hadn't pushed for more information. He assumed if Becca had taken some time off or gone out of town that was her business. He also suspected the time away from one another would be good for both of them. But damn, if he didn't miss her.

"Don't you think that's strange?"

"Rebecca works hard. Taking time off is her prerogative."

Liz rolled her eyes. "What's wrong with you?"

"What do you mean?"

Her voice rose slightly. "You're acting as if her disappearing doesn't matter."

"You're exaggerating. She hasn't disappeared."

Liz shook her head in disbelief. "Don't you care about her?"

He ignored her question. He really did not want to discuss Becca with his daughter again.

Elizabeth harrumphed. "Ever since you slept with her, you've been acting weird. I had no idea you were like that. Men suck!" She stormed to the stairs.

"Wait just a minute!"

She turned to face him.

Travis stood up. "How did you know Becca and I—well, you know."

"I'm fifteen, Dad, I'm not stupid."

Great. Travis sank back into his chair.

Liz walked back toward him. "I thought you were different from other guys."

"What?"

"You got Rebecca into bed and now you're done with her. Men do it all the time. I just didn't know you were one of them."

"You're wrong. I'm just confused. Can't you understand that? And where have you been learning all this stuff?"

"On the bus, TV talk shows, magazines."

"That's it. From now on, you walk to school and they'll be no more afternoon TV or magazines of any kind!"

"No bus?" she shrieked. "School is almost a mile away."

"Start now, you'll be there by Monday."

She paused. Her voice was low. "Then what did you do to make Rebecca leave?"

"What makes you think I did something?"

Liz tilted her head and studied him.

Travis threw his hands up into the air. "Look, I haven't seen her since she stayed the night."

"And you don't think that's strange?"

"No. Not really. Rebecca likes her space. I've called and she hasn't returned any of my calls."

"Typical man."

"You're fifteen, hardly a specialist male minds."

"I know enough."

"She's pushed me away. All I can do now is wait."

Elizabeth thought for a moment. "You've given her time to think, so don't just sit here. Go to her."

Travis ran his hands through his hair and sighed. "It's not that easy."

"Why not?"

"I pushed too hard."

Elizabeth sat opposite him. "How?"

"I opened my mouth before I thought about what I was going to say."

"How?"

"I asked her to move in."

She smiled. "Here? With us?"

He frowned. "I don't know why I'm telling any of this to you."

"I love her, too. But even I've got to say, it was too soon for that."

Travis rubbed his temples. "I thought asking her to move in would be a good thing. Now I see that it was the worst thing I could have done."

"No shit," Liz mumbled.

"Don't swear."

She smirked at him. "Sorry." Their eyes met. Travis hadn't expected to see so much understanding in his daughter's eyes.

"So you admit it. You love her?"

Travis groaned. He had never planned to discuss his sex life with his teenage daughter. "None of that matters. She said no. I scared her." And I hope I didn't push her so far away that I can't get her back.

Liz shook her head in disbelief. "You know what I think?"

He didn't bother to answer. Like it or not, she was going to tell him.

"I think it's too much too soon, Dad. Sure, Rebecca wants the whole package. But after her first experience with you, did you really think she'd actually agree to move in here?"

Travis swore no matter how hard he tried, he'd never get used to the fact that this young woman sitting before him was his daughter. *He'd never done anything so perfect in his entire life.*

He walked toward the picture window in the kitchen and looked out.

"We talk every day, Dad. Rebecca and I know a lot about each other." She didn't even try to disguise the disgust in her tone.

Travis turned and studied his daughter. "It isn't possible. Not right now."

Liz stood and walked to stand beside him. "You just admitted you loved her. Are you telling me you're not in love with her?"

"I'm not sure." He wasn't lying. Right now, he wasn't sure of his name let alone his feelings.

"What is it with you?" Liz's voice cracked. "You have a commitment problem or something?"

That's it. He'd have the cable access removed from their television tomorrow. He shook his head in anger, "I will not discuss this with you."

She smirked. "Typical."

"What?"

"Men. You disconnect yourself when the subject turns around to focus on whatever it is you've done wrong."

"I have *not* done anything wrong. And do not place

me amongst your preconceived ideas about what men are like."

Liz headed toward the staircase. "They're not my ideas. Freud, Psychology 202."

Terrific. Who was the teacher here?

Before leaving she turned. "You realize I'm not getting any younger."

"What's that supposed to mean?"

She shook her head. "By the time you make up your mind about Becca, it might be too late. Do you really want to lose her again?"

"Hold on."

She stopped at the foot of the stairs at his directive and looked at him.

"How did you know about—?"

"It's a small town, Dad. A person can't burp without everyone knowing something."

****

After having his mind read by a fifteen-year-old, Travis needed a walk. Before he knew it, he wound up at Kate's Café.

Michelle was sitting in her booth in the back sipping a mug of something hot. The steam rose above her head like circles at the top of a chimney. She caught his eye and nodded for him to join her.

He strode over to her table. "Where is she?" He slid into the red vinyl booth. Travis' patience was wearing thin and he had to talk to her.

He saw merriment in her eyes. Great. She had him where she wanted him.

"I haven't the foggiest idea."

He leaned his head in his hands. "Yeah, right. You two don't wash your hands without telling each other.

She hasn't answered my calls. I need to talk to her."

Michelle put her mug onto the table and looked Travis in the eyes, "Do you realize if you spent half your time loving her, really loving her, rather than apologizing, you two might just be one of the happiest couples on the planet?"

A direct hit, below the belt. Travis blew out a deep breath. "Let me rephrase that. I want to tell her I was a fool. And I wish she'd come home."

"Better. Still, I can't help think it could use a little work."

Travis groaned. "There are other things I want to tell her."

"As long as they're things she wants to hear, and that you mean them." She laughed. "When I talk to her later, I'll relay your message. She's in Philadelphia at a conference."

So she hadn't left because of him? Thank God.

He stood.

"Wait. Not so fast." She motioned for him to sit down.

Uh. Oh. Michelle and Becca were best friends and when push came to shove, and she could shove, she didn't hesitate to let him know where she stood.

"I don't get it. You're crazy about her. Everyone sees that. What's stopping you two from getting together?"

"What if it doesn't work?" *What if this marriage falls apart like my first did after only three years?*

Her mouth dropped open. "You're joking, right?"

Travis shook his head.

"This is priceless. You're worried about your fictitious marriage to Rebecca ending, and she's worried about your ability not to commit."

"She is?"

Michelle nodded. "Why wouldn't she be?"

She had a point. He had left without so much as a goodbye. In his defense, what woman wants to hear that their boyfriend got another woman pregnant?

"Perhaps if the two of you focused on simply loving each other, you might live happily-ever-after once and for all."

Travis smiled into Michelle's blue eyes. She was amazing. "So you're saying—"

Flustered, she interrupted him. "Travis, do not analyze everything so much. Just tell her how much she means to you. Show her you've changed. That's all she wants."

"So this convention? Is it only a few days?"

Michelle nodded. "She should be back tomorrow."

Travis grinned. "I just worry about her, that's all."

"Me, too." Then she leaned in closer to Travis. "So understand this. If you hurt her again, I'll hunt you down and kick your ass."

Travis swallowed. Michelle wasn't just Becca's best friend, she was also a black belt in karate. Right now, this petite woman reminded him of his mother—a tiny lady he had known better than to ever disobey, a caring woman he had loved dearly and respected greatly but who could pin you up against the wall in two point five seconds without breaking a sweat. "I won't do that."

****

The next morning, during a break in the convention, Rebecca had listened to all of Travis's phone messages. She wished he would leave her alone.

In an effort to push him out of her mind, she erased every one of his voice mails. Unfortunately, that didn't help. She wished she could stop thinking of that night they had spent together. How perfect everything had been. Or was she just caught up in some romantic fantasy?

No. They had been great together. And she wanted nothing more than to spend the rest of her life making love to him night after night. Sadness crept over her. But that wouldn't happen. If Travis thought she'd slip into his bed whenever he invited her, he was dreaming. She was old-fashioned and sleeping with a man was something she did only when she cared deeply for them. In Travis' case she hated to admit it, but the word care didn't cover the multitude of emotions he stirred inside her. Against her better judgment she had fallen for him again. But Travis would never commit. And if he couldn't commit, neither would she.

****

Thursday, after work, Travis found a note on the kitchen counter from Liz. *Some of the neighbors said Rebecca left town. No one knows if and when she'll be back. Great job, Dad, looks like your terrific communication skills have her believing there's nothing worth coming back to Golden. Not even us. Liz.*

He approached his daughter's bedroom. Before knocking, he blew out a deep sigh. *He figured whatever crap she was about to give him, he had it coming.* He knocked twice but she didn't answer. Maybe she was sleeping. He turned the knob to check on her only to find her room dark and empty.

Travis checked his watch—nine-thirty, Liz's curfew on school nights. He walked back downstairs trusting in the knowledge that she would arrive home any minute.

At ten-thirty Travis couldn't tamp down his nerves any longer. He paced the living room like a wildcat searching for prey. The empathy he had felt an hour ago toward his daughter had turned to anger. Liz was setting him up. That's what she was doing. The damn kid loved to argue. And no matter how Travis told himself to calm down, it was impossible.

She needed a good lesson in consideration. When she got home, they would sit down and have an adult discussion. He was more than pissed at her irresponsibility to not even call him. She knew damn well he'd worry about her.

At eleven o'clock he contemplated calling the police. He had gone from pissed to scared shitless in less than an hour. Where the hell could she be? Instead of phoning the police right away, he called the homes of various friends he knew Liz had made since her move to town. Thank God he had insisted she write their names and phone numbers into his address book.

No luck with the phone calls. No one had seen or heard from her since earlier today. To make matters worse, she wasn't answering her cell phone. Funny, she answered it every time one of her friends called. Christ, she spent half her life text messaging. Couldn't she answer just one of his calls?

Travis' head spun. He watched the news, read the papers. It seemed as though every time he turned on the television news of another kid missing covered the screen, distraught parents in the background. This one walking to her friend's house, that one going to the mall, none of them ever returning home again.

And they were all babies usually no older than fifteen. Fear twisted his heart. Was anywhere safe for kids to go these days? Liz could be in some serious danger. Travis couldn't take this anymore.

He called the police.

Chapter Sixteen

As planned, Rebecca drove home from Philadelphia Thursday night. She recognized Travis' number on the display screen of her cell phone and ignored it. When the hell would he get it through his head that she didn't want to speak to him?

She had tried to spend some time thinking about their situation, but the convention, full of new products, had her on overdrive, and her issue with Travis easily pushed aside.

Her phone rang and she checked the screen. Travis could be so persistent it irritated her. Didn't she have the right to leave town for a day or two? Why was he the only one who got to travel on a minute's notice? After the third ring, her exasperation was beyond control. She turned off the phone and turned on the radio. He'd have to wait.

****

Travis left yet another voice mail on Becca's phone. Where was she and why wasn't she answering? Could a decorating convention still be going on at eleven o'clock at night? Random thoughts drifted through his mind. Could she be in danger too? Wasn't it bad enough his little girl hadn't come home yet? Did he have to start thinking bad thoughts about Becca, too? His irritation grew as the doorbell rang.

The police had arrived.

****

Rebecca stopped for gas at the next rest stop. While the gas pumped into her tank she turned her phone on. Michelle had asked her to call when she got home. Already eleven o'clock, Rebecca didn't want to call any later. A minute later, Michelle picked up.

"Hi, it's me."

Michelle's sleepy voice made Rebecca cringe.

A television played in the background. "I'm sorry. I woke you."

"No. It's perfectly fine. I dozed off while we were watching the news. Are you home yet?"

Rebecca looked down the empty road. "I stopped for gas. I should be there in forty-five minutes, depending on the snow. I didn't want to call you any later than this. We'll talk in the morning. Go back to sleep."

"Becc?"

"Yeah."

"Travis was looking for you."

"So?"

Michelle cleared the sleep from her throat. "You two need to talk."

Rebecca sighed. "I have five missed calls from him on my cell."

"Trust me on this. Call him back."

"It's late."

"Stop making excuses and call him!"

"Fine. Relax, will you?"

"Tell me what he says tomorrow."

"I will. And Michelle?"

"Yeah?"

"Thanks."

Rebecca stood staring at the phone in her hand. When it rang again she jumped. His name displayed on the front of the phone. Travis.

"Becca?"

"Yes."

"Thank God."

He was out of breath.

"What's wrong?"

His voice cracked. "Liz is missing."

"Are you sure?"

"Yes."

"Call the police."

"They said unless she's had been missing for twenty-four hours, there was little they could do."

"Maybe she's just running late."

"She said she was going to the movies with Ali."

"Okay, well maybe they met friends who had a car and it ran out of gas."

"I called Ali's house. She's home and had no plans to see Liz tonight. Look, I know I'm the last person you want to see right now, but would you stop by my place when you get back?"

She could hear the distress in his voice and hated to think he was going through this alone, so she pushed all the bad feelings she had for him aside. This was about Elizabeth. She was missing, and Rebecca wanted to find her just as much as Travis. So she said, "Of course," and disconnected the call.

She hadn't planned on seeing him so soon. But this wasn't about her and Travis. All she could think about was Elizabeth and that she could be in trouble. Rebecca detached the gas pump and paid with her credit card. Grabbing her receipt, she slipped into the driver's seat and locked the doors. Then she started the engine and cranked up the heat. Her mind raced.

Where could Elizabeth be? At a friend's house? No. Travis had said he called all her friends. *Oh dear God please let her be safe.* Rebecca had grown more than fond of her. The two of them had a connection. She had grown to love Elizabeth like she was her own child.

Pulling her car back out onto the highway, realization dawned. Peter's Peak. The old cave at the top of Mount Golden. Why hadn't she thought of it before? Elizabeth was up at Peter's Peak with Christian. She had to be. She told Rebecca she and Christian went there to talk if either of them was upset about something.

Rebecca grabbed her cell but hesitated to call Travis. He would have a cow when he found out where she was and who she was with. Still, Rebecca knew how strong-willed Elizabeth was and she couldn't ignore the hunch that Peter's Peak was where they'd find her. She also knew she'd be breaking her word to Elizabeth.

But right now Rebecca knew she had no choice. *Elizabeth could be hurt.*

Alone.

In trouble.

No. She was the adult and couldn't worry about breaking a promise to a teen who wouldn't understand what her father was going through. Elizabeth's safety was at stake so Rebecca pushed all thoughts of Elizabeth and the aftermath she might have to deal with once the child was found.

She dialed Travis' cell. He picked up immediately.

"I think Elizabeth is at Peter's Peak."

"What?"

"She told me it's where she and Christian go when they what to be alone to talk."

There was silence on the phone line. "Even though I forbade her from seeing him again?"

"Yes. Even though you forbade her. Travis, she thinks with her heart. She's a romantic. I realize you're all grown up now, but there was a time when you would have done the same thing." His non-rebuttal reinforced her belief that she was right. "Just go, Travis. I have this feeling that's where they are. Besides right now do you really care where she is? Isn't the fact that she be found safe and sound the priority here?"

Travis sighed. "You're right." Then he asked, "Becca. How did she know about Peter's Peak?"

Her mother's words came back to haunt her. Sweetheart, you can be so naïve. "Don't be so naïve. Generations of kids have been using Peter's Peak as their place. We weren't the only kids to ever go up there and make out."

"Oh, great."

"Look. You must remain calm when you find her. You can't go crazy and lose your temper. Nothing will be accomplished with an argument."

"Jeez, Becca, I told her I didn't want her with that Christian kid, anymore. She stays out two hours past her curfew and I'm not supposed to raise my voice?"

"Absolutely not. It's important you stay calm. A cooperative front will do you more good than harm."

He sighed loudly. She was right. Damn. Sadly, this woman knew his daughter better than he did. "Okay. I'll leave right after I talk to the police."

"No. Wait there for me. Please."

"I'll try."

She disconnected the call and spent the rest of the ride praying that Elizabeth and Christian were safe and hadn't done anything they weren't ready for.

Rebecca was only half way home when she sensed trouble. The weather report on the car radio claimed snow continued to fall at the rate of four inches an hour and even with her windshield wipers set on high, visibility was next to nothing. She checked the clock in the car. *Unless she had a cape in the trunk that gave her the power to fly, it would take forever to make it in forty-five minutes.*

Finally, an hour and a half later, Rebecca pulled up outside Travis' Victorian. Irritation roiled at the man who had a one-track mind. Why couldn't he just listen? His car was gone. He hadn't waited.

Thickheaded bull.

Frustrated, she pulled her cell from her purse.

She'd drive to wherever he was and meet him there. She wanted to be there when he found Elizabeth. "Where the hell are you?"

Travis' voice cracked when he said, "At the hospital. Liz has been in an accident."

"I'm on my way." Panic gripped her. Everything seemed to happen in slow motion like it does in a movie after that. With shaking hands she drove to the hospital. *Dear God, please let her be all right.*

The hospital entrance was a vivid white and smelled like disinfectant. Rebecca wrapped her arms around herself in an attempt to rid herself of the chills that bombarded her. Nausea enveloped her as she silently prayed that the teen who in a few short weeks had become more to her than she cared to admit would survive.

Harsh fluorescent lights overhead caused her to shield her eyes. After giving the nurse at the station Elizabeth's name the nurse said, "I'm sorry you can't go back there unless you're—"

"Family," Travis responded from behind both of them.

"Not to worry," he reassured the nurse. "She's family."

"All right, Mr. McGill."

"Where is she?" Rebecca's mouth was dry like cotton.

"In surgery. Come on, I'll take you to her room."

"Surgery?" Oh no. Please let her be okay.

He nodded as he led her to the elevator. "She needs stitches. You were right. They were on their way to Peter's Peak. The police found them."

"She got hurt? How?"

He nodded. "She had a pretty bad fall."

Rebecca's stomach turned. "And what does the doctor say?"

"He says she'll be fine. Seems she suffered a nasty concussion when they tried to descend the mountain on foot. What were they thinking? If the car wouldn't start, they should have just sat there until we found them."

"Kids don't think like we do. They were probably scared. It was snowing pretty hard. I'd want to get off that mountain fast too."

"Still, no matter what the doctor says, I won't believe Liz is really okay until I hear her voice. When I got here she was unconscious. When they wheeled her into surgery, it broke my heart."

He slid his hand along the middle of her back. She leaned into his grip. On the way up in the elevator to Liz's hospital room, Travis explained what had happened. Angry with Travis, Liz talked Christian into going up to Peter's Peak so they could talk. When the weather turned worse, they decided they had better head home. On the way down the mountain, Christian's car stalled. The two of them decided to walk the rest of the way. Liz slipped and hit her head on a rock. Christian called 911, the police found them, and they brought them here.

"So when did you find out all of this?"

"A short while after you and I hung up. I was so out of it I just came here." He ran his hand through his already mussed hair.

His eyes were full of remorse. "I'm sorry, Becca."

Rebecca reached up and pushed a few stray hairs back for him. Their gazes locked. "She's going to be okay. I know she will."

He swallowed and nodded. "I don't know what I'll do if I lose her."

"We're not going to lose her."

****

In the wee hours of the morning, while Travis waited for Elizabeth to come out of surgery, he glanced down at Becca sleeping in his arms. They were sharing a loveseat in Liz's room waiting for her to emerge from surgery. He didn't know what he would have done if she hadn't come here to be with him. He also didn't know how he'd managed without her all these years. Strangely enough he didn't find himself thinking back to when they were younger, the times they had shared.

Instead, he found himself thinking about the

present and the life he had built for himself and Liz here in Golden, his newly renovated house, and his friends. Especially the most important friend curled up soundly in his arms.

Like a switch turning on in his head, Travis had never been more sure of his feelings for Becca and how they'd grown since he had arrived in Golden. Watching her sleep, it occurred to him that he never wanted her to be far away from him again. That realization led to another more important one. One he should have acknowledged weeks ago but had been too blind or perhaps just too stubborn to admit. He loved her and he'd do whatever was necessary to keep her in his life, and by his side.

He brushed the hair from her forehead and kissed her. "I love you, Becca."

****

Rebecca lay absolutely still in his arms. Why was it so hard for him to tell her face-to-face how he felt? She just heard him proclaim his love and yet she couldn't take him seriously. He had whispered it to a woman he thought was sleeping. She wanted, no needed, to hear it when she was awake. Eye-to-eye, so she could sense it in his touch, feel it in his kiss, see it in his eyes.

Her heart sank with the realization that he would probably never tell her. And that wasn't good enough for her. She wanted, no she deserved, someone who believed in her and their relationship. Someone who wouldn't be afraid to tell the woman he loved just that. Face-to-face. No matter what the outcome.

Travis had never been one to take chances. And sadly, Rebecca was certain his insecurities would have him doubting the validity of his statement. More importantly how would she handle it if he said it, and then realized he didn't mean it as deeply as she? Even though all these years had come and gone, she knew she couldn't handle that much pain again. Why she had ever let herself get involved at all dazed her. But she had learned long ago that when it came to her heart and Travis McGill, she had little control.

Laying in his arms now, dread swept through her. Sooner or later she'd have to pretend to wake up. Step out of the contented, warm glow his arms wrapped protectively around her caused, and deal with the reality. The reality that no matter how much she loved him, Travis would never fully return her love.

****

Elizabeth was wheeled out of surgery and transferred into her room at four a.m. The thud of the gurney entering the room and the hospital staff lifting and moving Liz into her hospital bed woke Rebecca who'd fallen back to sleep in Travis' arms.

Dazed, she sat up and shivered. *What time was it?* She watched the workers who had moved Liz silently slip out the door. Travis rushed to the side of his daughter's bed. His love and concern for Elizabeth brought tears to Rebecca's eyes.

Looking at Elizabeth lying there, her head wrapped in gauze bandages, she looked so little and frail. All Rebecca wanted to do was protect her. Wake her and tell her she loved her. Instead she wrapped her arms around herself and backed away. Travis leaned his head onto the bed, holding Elizabeth's small hand tightly in his and whispered words of encouragement and love to his daughter.

Rebecca swallowed hard. The two of them were

together. That was all that mattered. Whether she and Travis worked things out wasn't important anymore. Elizabeth needed her father and Travis was exactly where he should be.

Outside at the nurse's station there was a slight murmur of hellos and goodnights being exchanged. They were changing shifts. Rebecca gave these women a lot of credit, and admired their strength, kindness, and fortitude. Dealing with sickness and death on a daily basis and still having the ability to smile was beyond inspiring.

They were angels here on earth.

****

Travis remained at Elizabeth's side as the hours dragged into late morning. Rebecca couldn't stand it any longer—the quiet, the waiting, the inability to help in any way, drove her insane. In an effort to comfort Travis with a hot cup of coffee, she stepped into the elevator and visited the cafeteria.

Upon entering the large dining room real life sprang into action right before her eyes. The clang of silverware, the brightness from overhead fluorescent lights, the splashes of laughter and conversation all managed to snap Rebecca from the quiet daze she'd been in since last night. The lines extended toward the door she had just entered.

Taking a tray she quickly slipped behind a large man with a white jacket and stethoscope hanging from his neck. Glancing around, more people than not had stethoscopes around their neck. *Great.* She'd chosen what appeared to be one of the cafeteria's busiest times to complete a simple errand she'd hoped would only take a few minutes.

Returning a short while later with two coffees, she found nothing had changed. Travis was still sitting by Elizabeth's bedside holding her hand. When Rebecca joined him, he looked up. Sadness encased his brown eyes. Her heart broke for him. No matter how much this man hurt her, she hated seeing him suffer.

"Still sleeping?"

Rebecca handed him a coffee. "She needs her rest. I spoke to one of the nurses at the desk, it's absolutely normal."

He nodded and opened the lid to sip from the hot liquid. "Time certainly drags when you don't want it too. I wondered where you went."

He did? She would have thought he hadn't even noticed she'd slipped out. "I thought we could both use a fuel injection."

His smile was forced. Rebecca knew he was exhausted. She also knew he would turn down the offer a nurse had made, but she went ahead and conveyed it anyway. "There is a vacant bed next door. Why don't you lie down? I'll wake you the moment she opens her eyes."

"No. I can't. Not until she wakes up and I know she's okay."

Rebecca sipped from her coffee. *Of course he couldn't.*

Wouldn't.

Not when Liz might wake at any moment.

Chapter Seventeen

Right before noon, Liz woke up. Rubbing her eyes she focused on the first face she saw. Travis' eyes filled with happiness and glazed with tears.

"Dad?"

He smiled and his voice cracked. "The one and only."

Looking into his little girl's eyes, he blew out a deep breath of relief. He kissed her cheek and held tightly to her hand. "I was so worried about you." He couldn't imagine his life without her in it. Nor did he ever want to.

"I'm sorry."

"Not now," he said. "We have plenty of time to talk when you feel more like yourself."

Rebecca walked to the opposite side of Elizabeth's hospital bed and gently squeezed her hand. "I'm so glad they found you. I had a feeling that's where the two of you were."

Pain and anger flanked Elizabeth's face as she ripped her hand from Rebecca's. "How could you?"

The young girl's gaze sliced through her.

"How could she what?" Travis asked.

Liz locked her attention on Rebecca. "You lied."

"Elizabeth, listen to me, please." Rebecca pleaded.

"Why? So you can lie some more?"

"Liz, stop it."

"She's not herself, Travis," Rebecca offered.

"I'm fine," Elizabeth snapped.

"If it hadn't been for Rebecca, I'd never have known where the two of you were."

"You're wrong. If it hadn't been for Christian calling 911 before I passed out—"

"Does it really matter who did what? You're safe. That's all that is important now." Travis gripped the railing on the bed.

The door to Liz's hospital room swung open and a tiny nurse entered carrying a tray with what looked like lunch. She placed it on the bedside tray and turned it in the direction of Liz.

"Look, we're all tired. Why don't you eat and we'll come back later," Travis said.

Liz harrumphed and pushed the tray away.

"Sooner you eat, sooner you can go home," the nurse advised.

Liz pulled the tray back. "It's a conspiracy."

Travis kissed Liz's cheek and shot a glance at Rebecca that said, we should leave. A moment later, they slipped into the hall. Christian had returned to the hospital and paced the hallway outside Liz's room like a lion in too small a cage.

****

"What did you think you were doing?" Travis snapped.

Christian cleared his throat. "It was my idea to go up to Peter's Peak, sir."

"I bet it was."

"I didn't realize just how bad an idea it was until the snow started falling so hard."

"I told you to stay away from my daughter." Travis

pointed at the boy who stood only inches away.

Christian gulped. “I’m—I’m sorry?”

Rebecca took Travis’ pointed finger and pulled him away from the teenager who looked about ready to faint.

“Travis. Let him explain.”

The look he shot Rebecca was one of shock. “Explain what?”

Rebecca nudged Christian. “I’m sure he has more to say.”

With Elizabeth more than angry with her she figured the least she could do was to help Christian. Rebecca knew Elizabeth cared for him and that he had never meant her any harm. Travis needed to hear that from this boy especially since Rebecca knew no matter what her father said, she’d continue to see Christian.

“I do?” the teen squeaked.

She frowned at him. “Yes.”

“Right, I do.”

“Why are you helping him?”

“I’m not, but I would like to hear the story from his point of view. Wouldn’t you?”

Travis grumbled under his breath.

Rebecca jutted her chin forward signaling Christian to continue.

“I figured it was more dangerous to try and continue up the mountain when my car stalled, and since our cell phones weren’t getting any signals, we decided—Liz decided, we should head down on foot.”

The young boy sank into one of the hospital’s plastic chairs. He placed his head in his hands. “I told her to let me go ahead of her. I wanted to be in front to protect her.” The boy swiped his eyes with his sleeve.

"She wouldn't listen. She just wouldn't listen."

Rebecca bit her bottom lip and shot Travis a sympathetic look.

Travis unclenched his hands.

Rebecca imagined Travis wanted to yell. But the young boy's eyes spoke the truth and showed nothing but the deepest concern for Elizabeth and guilt that he hadn't been able to prevent her accident.

Travis leaned over and consoled the boy. "Don't be so hard on yourself. I know you had her best interests in mind. That girl is as stubborn as a bull."

The bewildered teenager looked up at Travis.

Travis tipped his head. "Come on, I'll buy us all lunch."

Rebecca watched Travis place a hand on the teenager's shoulder and lead him toward the cafeteria. Her heart more than warmed. No only had he made great strides with Elizabeth since they had moved to Golden, now he was comforting her young man. What the hell would he do next?

****

That night Rebecca phoned Travis. When he'd dropped her off at her place, he insisted he would be by early tomorrow morning. He wanted Rebecca to go with him to pick Elizabeth up from the hospital. Tossing the idea over in her mind, Rebecca thought otherwise. Upsetting Elizabeth further wouldn't do anyone any good. She needed a few days to cool off—to recuperate from the accident, to think things through.

"You should pick up Elizabeth by yourself tomorrow." She blurted into the receiver as soon as Travis answered.

"What? Look, if you're worried about her giving

you attitude, don't be. She's over her mood, trust me."

"I am not worried about any such thing. Besides, that's not the point."

"Then what is?"

"The two of you need some time alone. She's gone through a lot over the past few days. She might want to talk about Christian, the accident, I don't know, anything. And if she wants to open up to you, there shouldn't be anyone else there to stop her."

"Since when does she talk to me about boys? She saves all that for you, remember?"

She did. Only too well.

All the afternoons of heart-to-heart talks with Elizabeth flooded back causing Rebecca's throat to tighten. No matter how close they had been over the past few weeks, Elizabeth was right. Rebecca had broken her word. And even though it had been the right thing to do, the only thing to do, Rebecca doubted a fifteen-year old would fully understand.

"Yes, I remember. Still, you should go alone."

Travis was relentless. "I'm coming by at nine. Be ready."

Rebecca felt her pulse race. He wasn't listening to her. He wasn't grasping what she was trying to tell him. "No."

There was pause on the other end of the phone. His voice was low and gravelly. "Will you at least come by the house for a visit?"

Rebecca rubbed her temples. Her head had been throbbing all morning.

"Becca—"

"I'll try," she whispered.

****

Back home, Travis peered into Liz's closet crammed with clothes. His mind spun. Cecile had sent the rest of Liz's things. When the boxes arrived, there had been more than he expected so like a good dad, he had offered to help Liz unpack thinking she would want to get it over with. Wrong.

Liz had refused help, insisted she could do it by herself, and nicely closed her bedroom door in Travis' face. So he backed off and quietly retreated downstairs.

Visions of her private undergarments hanging in the laundry room a few days ago still haunted him. He was having a very hard time admitting that his little girl was no longer a little girl. So here he was standing in the middle of hormone hell, staring at the closet as though he'd never seen one before. Did every teenage girl own this much clothing?

Get your shit together, Travis, his internal voice screamed. He raked his hand through his hair and began searching for a pair of jeans. The fall on Peter's Peak had ripped Liz' jeans beyond repair along with her favorite blue jacket, and dried blood had ruined her shirt. Liz needed some clean clothes to wear home from the hospital. He grabbed a pair of jeans and a plaid shirt and tossed them into a duffel bag. He'd seen Liz wear both multiple times and figured they'd do.

God, he wished Becca were here. She could retrieve whatever Liz needed and he would wait downstairs. It just felt wrong for him to be looking at Liz's personal things.

Slowly he opened Liz's top dresser drawer. Grabbing the first bra and panties he saw, he shoved them into the duffel. There were clean socks on her bureau so he confiscated a pair. He blew out a deep breath. Thank God that was done.

On his way out of her room, he took her favorite beige suede boots. It had snowed again last night and she would definitely need them. Slipping into his own winter jacket he realized Liz's light blue ski jacket they had bought on their first shopping trip together was blood stained and no doubt ruined. He'd have to fix that. There was one more stop he needed to make before heading to the hospital.

****

Inside the teen's hospital room, the television blared. Travis took it as a good sign. His daughter was on her way to a full recovery. A tray of untouched food sat next to her bed.

"Not hungry?"

Liz shrugged. "I want to go home."

He sighed. At least she was calling their place home now. The look on his daughter's face told him not to push. Becca's not being here upset him. But it devastated Liz. Travis held up the bag he'd packed for her. "I brought you clean clothes and signed all the release forms. As soon as you're dressed, we can go."

His daughter's bottom lip quivered. "I'm sorry."

Travis rushed to her and drew her into his arms. "I'm sorry, too."

"Rebecca hates me and probably the two of you will never—"

"Never what?"

"Get together, marry, and live happily ever after."

"Is that what you want, Liz?"

"It is if you want it."

Damn straight that's what he wanted.

As realization of his deep love for Becca trickled

through him so did his gratification for a daughter like Liz. He was such a lucky man to have two loving women in his life.

He handed her tissues from her bedside tray. “Honey, she doesn’t hate you.”

“I called her a liar. She was only trying to help.”

“We all say things we don’t mean when we’re upset. Now you see there are some times when a person just can’t keep their word. Especially when it comes to the safety of someone they love.”

Elizabeth whispered, “I know that. Now anyway. And Mom—” The teenager sobbed. “All this time I’ve been mad at her when she was just trying to be there for me. She was always there for me.”

Travis leaned in and kissed his daughter’s forehead. “Your mom was in an accident. No one could have stopped it from happening.”

“I miss her,” Liz whimpered.

“I know, honey, I know.” *He suspected she always would.*

She swiped at both eyes with her free hand. “I miss Rebecca, too.

“So do I. If Becca isn’t here, she has a good reason and I guarantee it has nothing to do with you.”

****

That afternoon after he and Liz got home, Travis stood beside the stove and stirred a pot of simmering chicken noodle soup. Canned soup would have to do until he had time to whip up the real thing. Liz hadn’t eaten anything at the hospital, so he was more than thrilled when she asked for soup.

Even though she had insisted she could come down into the kitchen and eat, he refused to allow it. He had every right to spoil her while she re-cooperated.

Placing the soup, buttered crackers and juice on the tray table next to Liz, he smiled. The color had returned to her face and she had even napped for a short while this morning.

"Did you eat?"

"I had a late breakfast."

She nodded.

"What's the matter? Soup too hot?"

She stirred the bowl. "No. It's great."

When she looked up at him he wasn't prepared for the sadness in her eyes. "Then what is it?"

"Why hasn't Rebecca come over to visit? I told you she was mad at me."

He didn't know. He suspected she had been detained. Curiosity niggled at him. Becca loved Liz. She'd never stay away on purpose knowing Liz would be hurt. Travis knew there had to be another reason. A good one. Becca wasn't a hurtful person.

"Nonsense. She spent the whole night with me at the hospital waiting for you to come out of surgery."

Liz shrugged. "I hurt her."

So had he. Travis sat on the edge of Liz's bed. "Rebecca is a grown woman. She would never hold that against you. Trust me honey, she just has a lot on her mind. You know she hates letting anything sit on her desk as long as she is able to address it."

"Maybe."

Not thinking about anything but making Liz feel better he added, "I'm sure she'll come by as soon as she can. Now, eat your soup. I'll be downstairs on the computer. Then I'm going to run out and do some errands."

Before he reached the door, Liz said, “Dad, thanks for my new jacket, you’re the best.”

Travis smiled. He had stopped at the Ski Barn before heading to the hospital and purchased a brand new blue ski jacket with fluffy trim around the hood. The duplicate of the one he and Liz had bought together.

He knew how much she loved that jacket. He would buy her anything that she asked for as long as she smiled at him like that. “You’re welcome. And you’re pretty wonderful too.” Then he turned and left.

After checking on Liz and making sure she had a tall glass of something to drink, Travis brought her tray downstairs. She assured him she would be fine while he ran an errand.

On the walk to Becca’s, his stomach roiled. He hadn’t been this nervous since, he couldn’t remember when, but all of a sudden he felt seventeen all over again. He silently scolded himself. This was Becca. He had nothing to be nervous about.

Yes he did. She held his future in her hands. To live without her would be torture and he knew he needed to prove to her once and for all that he had changed. That he was no longer the kid who acted before he thought. That he was a man who knew what he wanted and was willing to wait for it. No matter how long it took.

Chapter Eighteen

Rebecca didn't expect to see Travis standing there when she opened the door. She had been expecting the delivery kid from the pharmacy with her medicine—a decongestant that was supposed to help her breath better. Or worst case scenario, she figured it could be her mother. Although she assured her she called the doctor and medicine was on its way, Rebecca wouldn't put it past her mother to rush over and start a pot of chicken soup.

It was laughable really. Everyone Rebecca worked with had the flu, why had she been so gullible, thinking she couldn't, wouldn't catch it. Letting herself get run down, not sleeping enough, why she hadn't taken a vitamin in over a week. What had she expected?

A quick phone call to her doctor this morning confirmed her diagnosis. A hundred and two fever, body aches, chills, sore throat. She was a mess. He had advised her to get bed rest and told her he'd call in a prescription for her congestion to the local pharmacy.

For a moment, she stood there staring at Travis, her head foggy and her mind full of cotton as Sherlock barked with delight and tried to break from her grip. She wiped at her red swollen nose with another one of those tissues that claims to contain lotion to sooth one's sore peeling nose. Yeah, right.

With each one of Sherlock's barks her head

throbbed harder. Have at him, boy. She placed the dog on the floor then pulled her robe tighter around herself and went back inside to her soft, comfy sofa where her pillow awaited her. She barely had the energy for that, never mind argue with Travis. Besides, he wouldn't have listened if she insisted he leave—he was too headstrong.

Just her luck, here she was dressed in sweatpants and an old sweatshirt, and Travis looked well, he looked sexy and attractive. *Damn him.* She pulled another tissue from her robe pocket and blew her nose.

Heck, she was sick and not in the mood for a visit from anyone. Least of all him.

She needed to lie down before she fell down. Cuddling on the sofa under her soft comforter she had brought down from her bedroom, she said, "I would have come over to see Liz—"

Travis finished for her, "You're sick. Jesus, Becca, why didn't you call me?"

His brow furrowed which meant he was pissed. She could care less. She could barely think.

He reached over and fluffed the pillow behind her head and felt her forehead with his lips. A hard, bone-wracking chill shot through her. Somehow she doubted it was from the flu. She leaned into him for warmth. He smelled so good.

"Babe, you're burning up. Let me take you to the doctor."

Rebecca shook her head. Then stopped. She shouldn't have done that. Her head spun round and round. She gripped her head with her hand. "Oh I don't feel good."

"Come on, we're going to the doctor."

She pushed his arm away. "No. I don't have to."

"Yes, you do." He pulled harder.

"Please. Stop."

He let go of her arm, but didn't give up. "A fever is serious. Why won't you let me take care of you?"

"I'll be fine. I already called my doctor. You don't have to fuss over me."

He knelt beside the sofa. "Yes, I do. We fuss over the ones we love when they're sick. Let me fuss over you."

"What did you say?" Rebecca swallowed hard because the sincerity in his eyes just about undid her. She'd been waiting for him to say those words for weeks. Why then didn't they thrill her now?

Because Travis lived only lived day to day, that's why—maybe he thought he loved her, but in a few weeks he'd probably change his mind. Besides, right now he just felt sorry for her. Even she knew she was a sad, pathetic sight.

She blew her sore red nose. She couldn't speak, her head throbbed, her ears popped, and her chest ached.

"I love you."

She shivered and he pulled her closer. He wrapped the comforter around her shoulder. "I understand. You don't believe me. Why in the hell would you? In the past I've lied to you, I've hurt you, and I abandoned you." His voice cracked. "I don't deserve your love now and I didn't then. But I love you with every ounce of my being and I'll do whatever's necessary to make you love me back. Let me make you some tea." He started to get up.

Rebecca grabbed his hand and stopped him. Overwhelmed by his honesty, a tear ran down her cheek. Could this really be happening? Had he changed and become the man she wanted? Needed more now than ever? "You love me?"

Travis leaned over and wiped the tear from her cheek. "Yes, and I'll tell you over and over again, if you need me too. I will never leave you again. I swear."

She could get used to hearing him say I love you. "I love you too," she muttered. Her heart felt like it was about to burst. Tears rushed down her cheeks.

The shocked expression on Travis' handsome face told her he hadn't expected her reply. She pulled on his hand, and he sat next to her on the sofa.

"You love me, too, Becca? Are you sure, because I don't want to rush you. I want you to take your time and know in your heart it's real." He handed her the box of tissues from the coffee table.

She nodded and blew her nose for the millionth time today. "It's more real than anything I've ever felt. I never stopped loving you. Ever."

He leaned his forehead against hers and let out a long, deep sigh. When Travis had returned to town she had sworn she wouldn't let him break down the barrier she so neatly put in place. But she had been naïve to the power of his charms. She'd forgotten how one smile of his undid every bit of her restraint.

And over the past few weeks, seeing him with Elizabeth and spending time with him working on his renovation, Rebecca had viewed the man he had become. The man he was when they were together, when they were alone.

The touch he used only on her, the kiss he gave only to her, the love he expressed so openly to her.

And she liked what she saw. She more than liked

it—she loved the man he had become and she wasn't about to let him slip out of her life for a second time. When she was with him she felt whole, and she hadn't felt that way in much too long. She wanted a life with him. With Liz. She never wanted to lose him again.

He discarded the used tissue and handed her a clean one. "I will always love you, too." He bent in to kiss her and she stopped him.

"I'm sick. I don't want you bringing this home to Elizabeth."

Travis thought for a moment. He kissed her forehead instead. "You're right. But, oh just wait until you're well. I won't be able to keep that promise any longer."

The mischievous twinkle in his handsome eyes told her what she could expect from him when she was well, and she couldn't wait. Even now sick with the flu, she wanted him.

But right now, she'd have to settle for a hug.

"I promise not to rush you. We'll start over. Take as long as we need. I just want us to be together, that's all that matters," he said.

Tears of happiness flooded her cheeks and she nodded. Spending her life with Travis was a fairy tale come true. The idea of that fairy tale coming to be after all these years more than overwhelmed her. She held onto him tighter.

"Don't worry. We have the rest of our lives. And this time, we'll get it right. This time nothing will keep us apart."

Rebecca's heart ached, and it wasn't from her congestion. It was from the emotions inside her that Travis had set free. The emotions she'd thought she'd gotten over. The emotions only he could unlock. The emotions meant only for him.

Spending the rest of her life with the only man she ever loved?

Rebecca couldn't wait.

Epilogue

Two years later.

When the kitchen phone rang, Rebecca hurried across the room to retrieve it from its cradle. At seven months pregnant, she waddled, rather than hurried, and found herself out of breath. Sherlock barked and jumped up and down. “Hush.” She hissed. He tilted his head and went back to his toys in the corner. Rebecca leaned back and stretched.

“Hi, it’s me,” Liz exclaimed.

“How are you, sweetie?” Rebecca asked. Her daughter had been away at college for only two months and the house seemed so empty, so quiet, without her.

“I’m great. How are you?”

Rebecca rubbed her protruding tummy. “Good. I’m good. A little winded. But good.”

The young girl’s laugh penetrated the phone. “How’s Sherlock?”

“Oh, he’s his normal barking self.”

As if he knew he was being talked about, Sherlock looked up from his rawhide toy and woofed.

“Where’s Dad? I tried his cell, but I only got his voice mail.”

Rebecca smiled. “You know your father. Ever since I told him I was pregnant he’s been working non-stop on the nursery. He probably left his cell in the garage. He was in a rush to get to the lumberyard to pick up some more wood before they closed for the day. He's making book shelves."

Liz's laugh permeated the phone line. "How does he feel about having a son?"

Rebecca smiled. "He's ecstatic."

"Of course he is. And so am I. I'm going to have a little brother. I can't wait."

Rebecca sighed. *Neither could she.*

"Tell him I'll call again later, okay?"

"Okay, honey. Be safe and take care."

"I will." Liz disconnected the call.

Rebecca replaced the receiver into its cradle and sighed. She glanced at the wedding band on her finger and silently thanked God for the many blessings he had bestowed on them.

It still felt like a dream that she and Travis were having a child. A child Rebecca didn't think she'd ever have. After losing Mike and Annie all those years ago, she'd thought her chance at motherhood was over.

But a few months ago, after a sweet love making session, Travis had convinced her that it was never to late if she still wanted to be a mother, and that it would be his pleasure to try and make her dream come true.

Besides, when he stressed how fun it would be to for them to try, over and over, well, she just couldn't resist his sexy charms. Only one month after attempting to get pregnant they'd succeeded.

The past two years together had been filled with nothing but happiness. And for that Rebecca couldn't be more grateful.

Travis burst through the back door, snapping her from her thoughts. "Hey, babe. Have anything for me to snack on?" He leaned over and nibbled her neck. "Besides you?"

Sherlock rushed to greet Travis.

"Hey, boy." Travis reached down and scratched the dog's head.

"I was just making you a snack when I was interrupted by the phone," Rebecca said.

"Who called?"

"Liz."

"Oh man. And I missed it?" He frowned. Travis tried to never miss a call from Liz. Since she'd gone away to school, they'd gotten closer and she called her dad every single night.

He fumbled through his pockets. "Where the heck is my cell?"

"I told her you probably left it in the garage. Don't worry, she said she'd call you back later."

He hit his head with the back of his hand. "You know me well."

Rebecca handed him his snack. "Uh huh. It was good hearing her voice. The house seems incomplete without her."

He leaned down and kissed her stomach. "Not for long."

Rebecca smiled. He was right. In two months their new baby would be here and their life together would change drastically.

Instead of quiet dinners and evenings filled with making love, their life would be filled with bottles, diapers, late night feedings and sleep deprived nights.

Rebecca smiled.

It was all she had ever wanted.

If you enjoyed *TRAINING TRAVIS*,
you'll want to try *MARRYING MR. RIGHT*,
author Cathleen Tully's Dearly Beloved story
released recently…

Missy Modesto had it all: a successful business, two fabulous kids, and a twenty-seven-year marriage to her high school sweetheart. But when too many arguments left them unable to compromise, she and Vinnie separated. Now, nine months later, their daughter is getting married and wants Missy to plan the wedding.

Vinnie Modesto is trying to put his life back together. He keeps in touch with his kids and is building his business to its full potential—something he should have done before the only woman he ever loved ended their marriage.

Missy dreads seeing Vinnie again, but when he arrives, eager to help with the wedding and offering solutions to every problem, Missy isn't sure what to think. Can she believe in the new man he's become during their separation? Or is this just another in a long line of Vinnie's empty promises?

A word about the author...

Cathleen Tully writes Sweet Romance, Contemporary Romance and Women's Fiction. Her first Contemporary Romance Novella, *MARRYING MR. RIGHT,* is available through The Wild Rose Press.

A Member of Romance Writers Of America, and the Liberty States Fiction Writers, Cathleen is a firm believer in honing her craft. A brown belt in Isshinryu karate, she loves the feeling of strength and independence it allows her.

Cathleen can be found on Facebook, and at www.cathytully.com. A born and bred Jersey girl, Cathleen lives in central New Jersey with her husband, Joe, and their two daughters.